GW00891780

Lament for Two Ladies

They couldn't have been more different. Ann Koppleman was an attractive, wealthy widow who lived alone in her beautiful California home—high on a hillside above the Pacific. Eugénie—just Eugénie—was a bag lady who slept rough and snatched a night's kip when she could in any empty room of the local hospital—something to which most of the staff turned a blind eye. Yet on the same night both women were murdered in identical fashion: by a slender knife efficiently plunged into the heart. What could they have in common, except, presumably the same killer? Detective Carl Pedersen set to work to find out.

His inquiries took him behind the scenes in Bay Cove Hospital, and into the lives (and secrets) of Ann's seemingly close family, but none of those who might be thought to have a motive for one of the murders had any motive for the other. Everybody was involved with everybody else, but nothing could be made to fit. Until a breakthrough item of evidence turned up and the missing piece of the jigsaw slotted into place.

by the same author

SOME DIE YOUNG
A PERSONAL POSSESSION

JEANNE HART

Lament for Two Ladies

COLLINS, LONDON

William Collins Sons & Co. Ltd
London · Glasgow · Sydney · Auckland
Toronto · Johannesburg

First published in the UK 1991

British Library Cataloguing in Publication Data

Hart, Jeanne
Lament for two ladies.—(Crime Club)
I. Title
813.54[F]

ISBN 0 00 232289 7

Photoset in Linotron Baskerville by
Rowland Phototypesetting Ltd
Bury St Edmunds, Suffolk
Printed in Great Britain by
William Collins Sons & Co. Ltd, Glasgow

For my sister, Patricia Ploughman

CHAPTER 1

Rod MacMillan shifted the folders he was carrying under his arm, balanced the styrofoam coffee-cup and reached for his key. He had come to the hospital early; none of the social workers had arrived, his secretary was not yet in. He planned to run through his notes for the meeting that day and glance over the material he had ready for Jean to type. The book was going slowly, but by evening, with Harriet's—demands, he thought, then amended it to needs—and with the two kids, he found he was too beat to put forth the effort. Maybe this business of coming in mornings would start things moving again.

Halfway through his coffee he remembered Eugénie. He had glanced into the empty room on his way down the corridor the evening before and thought he spotted her; then, carefully not looking in again, had slid the door shut and gone on his way. If the hospital needed the bed they'd evict her; till then, since the room would have to be cleaned again anyway, he might as well leave her.

He liked Eugénie. He had described her to Harriet. 'She may be a bag lady, but she has a certain elegance,' he said. 'She wears a hat, not a bad-looking one, and carries her things in this tapestry bag that must be left over from some other life, and she doesn't smell. She looks good, actually; she's straight, no osteoporosis. Maybe it's good for the body to keep moving the way she does.'

Eugénie had latched on to the notion of sleeping in an empty hospital bed some time ago. By now everyone at Bay Cove Hospital knew her. She was a sort of joke: her slyness and ingenuity at slipping in and finding just the spot where she was least likely to be discovered and her dignity on banishment from that spot. Most of the doctors regarded her with mild affection. Not Lew Mawson, of course; to him she was no joke. Of course, considering what had happened between her and Mawson, that was no surprise. Rod still felt uneasy knowing that, even though nothing would surprise him, coming from Lew. Lew had always struck him as a strange guy, very strange.

But the others would rout her out and then over coffee laugh about her and refer to her as 'our Eugénie'. No one was quite sure how they'd come to know her name. Someone or other must have talked to her.

For that matter Rod had talked to her. As head of Social Work he'd been called upon to find out what she lived on, whether she had a welfare cheque. Who she was, for Christ's sake. He had gotten no place.

Eugénie had sat in the chair opposite him, back flat, hands folded in her lap. Rod asked her name.

Eugénie.

Last name?

Just Eugénie.

Rod had straightened in his chair, aware he was slumping. Chatting her up to soften her defences seemed out of the question. He went to the heart of the matter.

Was she, that is, did she have some source of income? A monthly welfare cheque, for example?

No, no welfare cheque.

What, then, did she live on?

She smiled, a distant smile with something of self-satisfaction in it. She managed.

Nothing further could be gotten from her. She made no explanation of her need for a bed, no apology for borrowing one. After enduring a few more seconds of her silence, Rod gave up. To compensate her for his intrusiveness, he invited her to breakfast in the hospital cafeteria. Eugénie accepted and ate heartily, her manners impeccable. After she had finished a second cup of coffee she rose, gathered up her big tapestry bag, shook hands with her host and left.

Rod finished his own cup of coffee, feeling distinctly bettered.

Now, remembering her in the unused room, he crumpled his cup into the wastebasket and rose. Good idea to move her out before things got lively on the floor.

There was a moment of indecision as he determined which of the closed doors was hers. Opening the door softly, he prepared to be gentle, shake her awake and, without fuss, send her on her way. Her tall frame lay on the bed, somewhat sprawled. Quietly he moved in, then stopped dead. Projecting straight up from Eugénie's chest was a slender knife. It had been efficiently plunged into her heart, and Eugénie was no longer with them.

Ann Potter Ford Koppleman had spent the evening with her daughter. Suzanne lived ten minutes away and now that she had finally determined what her major would be, history, spent a good deal of time at her mother's, making plans for the present school year and generally talking things out. After the long period of rebellion, then the coldness, their relationship had improved. Sometimes Ann felt that if her other three children lived in Bay Cove, as did Sue, things would have gone smoother with her daughter. No matter what effort Ann put into not interfering, she found herself focused on Suzanne simply because Suzanne was the only child there. Out of sight, out of mind, had a certain truth to it.

Now, preparing for bed, Ann noted once again how much she relished her solitude. Growing up in a family of five, having four children herself, being married to Ernest, a demanding man who needed attention at every turn, had given her more than her share of togetherness. Now she relished the peace that settled over her when no one else was in the house. Even the problems that had plagued her lately seemed slighter without others around.

Not, she observed as she sat before her dressing-table mirror brushing her hair, an old-fashioned habit of which she had never broken herself, that she couldn't marry again if she wanted to. Ollie had never given up hoping. And she was an attractive woman. She leaned forward to examine her skin. Clear, not badly lined. True, a facelift would improve things, but she had not yet succumbed to that vanity. She tipped her head back and checked her throat. That was showing signs of age, but lately she resorted to colourful wrapped scarves and high-necked blouses with soft distracting bows tied beneath the chin. She sighed. Too bad one couldn't look as young as one felt.

But she was a lucky woman. Ernest had left her more than well provided for and now with her father's recent death, she had come into her inheritance. Actually, she had never been anything but well cared for, surrounded by comfort. The house in the prettiest section of town, not extravagant in size but more than adequate for her growing family and at present an affluence of space, still pleased her. She could not imagine moving into something smaller, a smart condo, for example. The children had suggested that she might be happier in a place with fewer memories, but now that her widowhood had advanced into its third year, she could not say the memories were painful. No, she was satisfied with life just as it was. She had her house, she had her work (she warmed at the recollection of all she had done at Marigold House and to further the University Garden Project), she had solitude. Peace. The children were fine. Really, all was right with the world.

She creamed her face, removing make-up, then applied a preparation which promised to decrease signs of ageing. She had bought a strap to encourage a lean line at the throat but on glimpsing herself in it had abandoned it. She had pride enough not to want to be found trussed up like that if she died in her sleep, an unlikely event.

She stood, casting a last glance at her figure in the lace-trimmed silk gown, and turned off all the lights except the bedlamp. Sliding into bed, she reached for her novel. It was a fascinating tale called *Ironweed*, with a vagrant as a protagonist. At first she had thought she would be unable to read it, so little identification did she feel with the character, but gradually she had become absorbed. After a while she found her eyes closing and she reached to turn off the bedlamp. Adjusting her pillow and pulling the blanket around her shoulders, she settled down to sleep, still on the far side of the bed, just as she had slept when Ernest was alive.

Stanley Potter discovered her.

They had planned to lunch. 'Let's meet at the Pelican,' he had said, 'we haven't eaten there lately. I'm ready for cioppino again.' They set the time for 11.30 to beat the crowd.

'Outside,' Stanley announced to the hostess. It was a clear, sunny day and tables were already beginning to fill on the glass-walled patio; he had come none too soon. 'And bring me a martini. Cold.' He relaxed in the balmy warmth of the Indian summer, aware of several eyes turned his way. He was a handsome man and knew it, but he was not vain. Glancing at his watch, he leaned back and waited for his martini. When it came, it was icy. One thing the Pelican knew how to do was make a fine martini.

At noon, still alone, he signalled the waiter to ask where phones were to be found. 'On her way, I guess,' he remarked to the waiter as he reseated himself; the fellow seemed to be lingering unnecessarily. 'Bring me another martini.' By 12.30, after another trip to the telephone, he was becoming uncomfortable about holding the table. The waiter was sympathetic. Too sympathetic. 'My sister,' Stanley explained. The waiter looked unconvinced and Stanley found himself wanting to insist. 'Must've got the wrong day,' he muttered. It sounded lame. He went ahead and ordered his cioppino.

Shortly after 1.30 he backed his grey Continental out of the parking lot. He was disturbed, uneasy. Looking at his watch he decided to detour, swing past Ann's. He cut around the Yacht Harbour, driving slowly past the boats with their marine blue flags, marking the hot little breeze and reflecting that if he weren't preoccupied with his sister, he'd be thinking this was the weather in which he most liked to sail. Gliding alongside the bay, noting the full beaches, not so full as they would be on the weekend, he turned off in the direction of Ann's. It was fifteen minutes before he pulled past the manicured golf course. A singular number of men his age seemed to be out. He wondered how they did it at this hour. He wound away from the course and down the hill, descending to the little road that led to Ann's place.

Her house stood mute. Digging for his key—like his brother and sister and Suzanne—he unlocked and went in without ringing. 'Anybody home?' he shouted. No one replied.

Walking through the house, he entered the living-room, went on into the dining-room and kitchen and then turned off to the bedroom wing. Her room was the big one at the end. The door was not quite closed. 'Anybody here?' he called, his voice more tentative now. An odd chill touched him. Then he pushed the door open and saw his sister where she lay in the last posture she had known in life.

Projecting from her chest was a slender knife which had been efficiently plunged into her heart.

CHAPTER 2

At the request of the hospital administrators, Detective-Sergeant Carl Pedersen and Detective Ronald Tate and their team arrived without fanfare. The corridor on which Eugénie's room was located had been cleared; with some explanation, a number of patients had been moved. Not enough beds were free to accommodate all those on the corridor, so the decision had been made to leave in place those who were bedridden, immobile, unlikely to move from their rooms. The corridor was blocked off to wanderers by strategically placed cleaning signs; and the crime scene team, along with the coroner's deputy, moved in quietly. With surprisingly little fuss surfaces were dusted, vacuums applied, measurements and photographs taken. By the time the room was ready to be sealed, things appeared essentially restored to normal in the rest of the hospital—shocked administrators and physicians back at desks and bedsides, flustered nurses busy once more with their duties. The body had been whisked away; at the unobtrusive removal of bodies the hospital was skilled.

Pedersen, standing in the empty room with his partner, surveyed what remained and turned up his hands. 'Our first bag lady. Who knows about bag ladies? Do we go down to the mall and cosy up to the street people?'

Tate shook his head. 'Did you see that knife?'

'Yes, a steak knife straight from Carson's. Label and all—he must have overlooked that. And no fingerprints.'

'The cut looked clean. You don't suppose one of the doctors sent her on her way?'

'I certainly hope not. That would complicate things no end. I'll be interested in what the post-mortem turns up.' He moved towards the door, looking at his watch. 'It's almost two. Let's seal this place and go talk with the social worker who found her. I imagine he's keeping himself handy.'

Rod MacMillan was in his office, the door open.

'Just a word,' Pedersen said. 'You found the woman?'

'Yes.' MacMillan seemed to be making his mind up about something. 'I noticed her in there last night and decided to leave her; closed the door, as a matter of fact. When I came in early this morning, I thought I'd send her on her way, let them clean the room.'

'Did you know her at all?'

'Not really. I knew her first name and that she wasn't on welfare. Since the—this happened, I've talked with one of the doctors. Jerry Cohen. A pædiatric cardiologist. It seems he ran into her in one of the rooms he uses for his patients and got a little more out of her than I did.' He smiled. 'So much for social work skills.'

'You didn't know her surname?'

'No, nor where she kept herself when she wasn't camping here. I've never seen her on the mall. Or at the public library. A lot of them hang out there. Of course I'm not down there very often.'

'There must be a community—they must know each other.'

Rod looked doubtful. 'I have no idea how much they communicate.'

Pedersen considered. 'Did she appear psychotic?'

'No, she seemed perfectly lucid when we talked. In complete command of the situation, in fact. But she may have had lapses. Some of them are in and out.'

'And this Dr Cohen?'

'He's just finished a cardiac catheterization. I know because it occurred to me you might want to talk to him. I called up there. Third floor.'

Dr Jerome Cohen was a tall, bone-thin young man with a mop of red-gold hair. Beneath his white coat he wore clean pressed jeans and below them white jogging shoes. He greeted them with an out-thrust hand and indicated chairs. His office was tidy and book-packed. He shifted an engagement calendar to the other side of his desk and leaned his elbows on it. 'Rod told me you wanted to see me. About Eugénie, I assume.'

'Yes.' Pedersen found that he was relieved at last to sit down. 'We hear you learned something from her, made friends with her.'

Jerry Cohen laughed. 'I'd hardly call it friends, that was one wary lady. But she relaxed a bit. Told me she'd been married. I tried to get out of her where her husband was, whether she had kids, but she clammed up again. But she did say she was divorced and after the divorce she wasn't well. I figured she'd had a psychotic break or some variation of one.'

'Did she mention hospitalization?'

'No.' He looked thoughtful. 'I—somehow I got the impression she wasn't hospitalized, but she didn't say. I don't know where the impression came from.'

'And you didn't learn her surname, either?'

'No. I asked. In fact I wanted her to try to get on welfare. Rod had already talked to her about it, but she seemed to have let down her guard with me that day, and I thought I might have some success. She froze up at the suggestion that she tell me her name. You know,' he added, 'I feel bad. She had a certain air about her. We'd all become quite fond of her. All except Lewis Mawson.' He laughed again.

'Lewis Mawson?'

'Maybe I shouldn't have said that. Lew's a psychiatrist, head of division here. He considered Eugénie the scourge of the planet. It offended his sensibilities to have her crashing in his hospital. That's Lew, he owns the earth.' His tone was dry.

Pedersen noted down the name. 'Maybe I should talk to him.'

'You can't now, he's at a meeting of division chiefs. Forget what I said. That was cruddy of me. He just didn't much fancy her sleeping in our beds.'

'What about the rest of the staff?'

'They kidded about her. She was clever. Never attracted attention coming in. By now, you'd have thought we could've spotted her. That bag she carried. Her hat. But somehow she slipped in and suddenly she was just there, asleep on one of the beds, easy as you please.'

The phone on his desk rang. Pedersen stood up to go, but before he and Tate could reach the door, Cohen called them back. 'It's for you, Detective. Headquarters.'

It was the lieutenant. 'Carl, I've had one fine old time tracking you down. Didn't you tell me when we talked earlier that this woman was killed with a steak knife?'

Pedersen was puzzled. 'Yes, why?'

'Describe it.'

'Nine or ten inches long, narrow blade, black handle. The only distinguishing feature was that there was a little black Carson's marker on it. Unobtrusive, the sort of thing you'd only notice if you were washing it, I suppose.'

'Well, it seems you'd better get over to—' there was a pause—'224 Wallace Place. There's been another murder, same sort of knife, sticker still on it. There must be some nut loose with a handful of knives.'

CHAPTER 3

After he hung up on the police, Stanley phoned his sister. She had spent an aimless morning, unable to settle to anything, drifting from the examination of a newly arrived magazine on the house and garden, to the desultory preparation of a lunch with which she played but did not eat, to the attempt to remove a spot from a favourite blouse. Kay usually read when she was at loose ends, but since her husband's peculiar non-return from his business trip, she had been unable to concentrate on a book.

The spot wouldn't budge. She tried lighter fluid. Left over. These days she seldom gave in to her urge for a smoke. Lighter fluid was usually magical when it came to spot-removal, but today it refused to work. Then, cautiously, she tried soap and water, wondering if she were setting the stain rather than removing it. She was holding the blouse to the light, trying to determine whether the spot was gone or merely obscured by leftover soap, when the phone rang.

It was Stanley. She must come immediately; Ann was dead, stabbed in her bed as she slept. Listening to him, she looked at the blouse in her hand; it had begun to tremble violently.

*

For a wonder, Roy was at home when Stan tried him. He had spent the morning at the museum but had stopped off home to pick up a batch of samples he had forgotten that morning. Having skipped lunch, when Stan's call came he was seated at a table in the kitchen, eating a sliced tomato and feta cheese sandwich wrapped in pita bread, the colour samples spread around his plate. He had just decided on the grey-green—it would be a subtle backdrop for the delicate Japanese-influenced paintings he was mounting—when the phone rang. He didn't answer it immediately; in fact he considered not answering it at all. Finally its insistence became irritating and he reached across the table to pick it up.

He must come at once. Stanley had discovered their sister Ann stabbed to death in her bed.

Roy's sudden movement tipped his coffee-cup and a puddle of liquid slowly spread, darkening the greys and greens and browns of the samples. He sat staring at the squares of posterboard as though he had never before seen them.

Wallace Place was a private road, unpaved, that meandered down a wooded hill. The house, half way along the hill, had turned its back to the wood behind it, facing instead towards the vista below where careful planning had created an unstudied effect: Japanese maples, clumps of brightness that could have been wild flowers, a little dry stream, stone steps and paths. Broad living-room windows looked out over the hill, and sliding glass doors fronted on a brick-paved patio on which several comfortable-looking chairs made of white-enamelled metal webbed with brown plastic were scattered informally as though a group of people had just risen and casually pushed them back. The house itself was low and long, one-storeyed, built of redwood that had weathered grey. It was a handsome building in a handsome setting. In its quiet and unpretentious way, it spelled money.

By the time Pedersen and Tate pulled into Wallace Place,

the family had gathered, clustered just inside the entrance hall as though unsure if they were welcome in their sister's living-room.

Pedersen took them in. Together they made a handsome group. Stanley Potter, the eldest of the lot, introduced himself. He appeared the most stricken. A good-looking man, dressed in a grey business suit, immaculate white shirt and dark tie, his face was white and drawn. In his glossiness he reminded Pedersen of some dimly remembered advertisement.

The younger brother put out his hand. 'Roy Potter.' In contrast to Stanley, he was slender and poetic-looking, with hair brushing the collar of his soft sports shirt, wearing snugly fitted jeans with a designer label over one buttock and sandals on his bare feet. He attempted a half-smile; he did not succeed.

Hovering nervously near the two men, the sister too extended a hand. 'I'm Kay Brennan, Mrs Brennan, Ann's sister. Are you . . . will you be . . .?'

'Yes. We'll be investigating.' He paused. 'This must be very hard for all of you.'

Her eyes filled with tears. Although she was certainly not out of her forties, a guess at her age was pointless. Her skilfully coloured hair was cut into a tumble of curls that appeared natural; she had removed her jacket, and her skirt smoothly emphasized the ungirdled line of her hip. Sheer dark hose and high-heeled shoes set off her fine legs. She had been crying, but the overall impression was subtly seductive. Even her face, flushed as it was with emotion, contributed to an effect of which Pedersen was sure she was unaware. He looked at her more closely. He wondered why, despite the chic clothing, the careful coiffure, the seductive façade, what came to mind was a lost little girl.

Pedersen murmured a few more words of sympathy and left Tate to accompany them into the living-room. He made his way back to the bedroom where the team was still at work. The body had not yet been removed.

He greeted Kramer, the detective in charge, and stood over the still figure. 'You know why I'm here?'

Kramer nodded. 'Harbison called. You had an identical MO on the murder of a bag lady this morning. At Bay Cove Hospital. He wants you on both cases.'

'Looks that way.' He glanced down. 'Somebody's leaving a trademark. Same type of knife. Same sticker—Carson's.'

Kramer nodded. 'I wonder if we're going to find more bodies around town.'

'He's democratic, at any rate,' Pedersen remarked. 'Picks from the social strata without discrimination.' Kramer grunted.

He looked around. Having just viewed Eugénie in her shabby blouse and jumper, with the worn tapestry bag and the tired hat the only evidences of individuality, he was struck by this body: the soft silk of the gown, now deeply stained, the rich bands of lace, the well-groomed hair and hands. And the luxury of the room. A champagne-coloured quilted satin spread had been carelessly pushed to the foot of the king-sized bed. Deep white carpeting stretched underfoot. A long dressing-table with strips of theatrical lighting was set against one wall. Jutting from another, next to glass sliding doors, stood a chaise-longue upholstered in white fur. It was the bedroom of a self-indulgent woman. He glanced back at her. A beautiful self-indulgent woman.

'How did the killer get in?' he asked.

'We aren't sure. No signs of forced entry.'

'She's alone? Was alone?'

'Well, we can't vouch for that, but she's a widow, the brother says. Widowed a couple of years ago and has lived here by herself since.'

'No alarm system?'

'There is one. Apparently she didn't turn it on at night. Only when she went out.'

Pedersen snorted in disgust. 'That makes a lot of sense. I wonder if she had a man. A lover. Someone who had a key or was here last night.'

'The bed—' Kramer began, but Pedersen nodded.

'Yes. Looks as if she was alone.' He sighed. 'Have you questioned the family?'

'Not really, yet. Maybe we'd better check and see who's in charge here. No point in my questioning them if you're going to be working on the case.'

'Right. I'll stroll in and ask about men friends while you check. I passed a phone someplace—oh, it's just out in the hall.' He paused. 'I don't think we ought to let anyone aside from the team see the sticker on that knife. Might as well keep the Carson name under wraps.'

'A lover?' Stanley was indignant.

Pedersen had put the question gently: Could your sister have been with a man at the time of her death? Stanley's reaction was that of an affronted son

Kay broke in. 'You don't know, Stan. Maybe she had someone. Do you know? Do you, Roy?'

Roy looked surprised. 'She wouldn't have discussed it with me. You'd have been the one she'd have told.'

Kay Brennan looked self-conscious. 'Maybe I'm wrong. She did say she was seeing a couple of men.'

'Ollie, I suppose,' Roy put in.

'Oh, Ollie. I didn't mean him.' She turned to Pedersen. 'Oliver Winter is an old friend of my sister's. He wanted to marry her when she was free—between marriages. I guess he'd still have liked to.'

Despite the fact that all three were distracted by shock, family relations and personalities were evident even in this small exchange, Pedersen noted. Stanley, conventional, protective of his sister, not too informed about her life. Kay, confidante of her sister, relaxed enough to be told about and accept the idea of lovers. Roy, the outsider? The detached one, of the family but not in it, the nonconformist?

'Your sister was married twice?' Pedersen asked Kay.

'Yes. She lost her first husband. The kids are his.'

'She had how many children?'

'Four. Their name is Ford.' Kay Brennan frowned. 'Suzanne lives here in town. We've called and called but we can't seem to get hold of her. Roy phoned the other kids, they're scattered all over the country. They're arranging to come.'

'Could Mr Winter have had a key to the house?'

'He might have, although I don't see why. She gave all of us in the family keys after Ernest died, and her kids, too. She seemed to feel safer knowing we could get in, I don't understand why.' She shook her head. 'It certainly didn't help. This happened.'

'Not just this,' Pedersen said. 'There was another murder today.' The thought that some killer was randomly stabbing women depressed him. 'It doesn't look good. Identical weapon and method.'

Three pairs of startled eyes turned towards him.

'Yes,' Pedersen said. 'The murders, of course, may not be connected. Or—' he paused—'they may be.'

CHAPTER 4

Pedersen located the daughter around dinner-time.

Suzanne Ford looked to be about twenty. In appearance, with her face free of make-up, her hair brushed back simply, dressed as she was in a blue jean skirt and long-sleeved white jersey, she might have been any student from the university. It was her self-possession that set her apart. She greeted Pedersen with a nod, waited for identification, then preceded him into her large living-room and indicated a chair. Her face was mildly puzzled. 'Did I park in the wrong place or something, Detective?' Her laugh was light, social.

The apartment she occupied struck Pedersen as luxurious for a college student. He accepted the chair she offered and she sat down opposite him. 'No, I'm afraid it's more serious than that,' he said gently. 'It's your mother. I'm afraid she's dead. She's been killed. Murdered.'

For a moment he thought she would faint; he half-rose from his chair. He had never grown used to telling family members of a death, never found a way, not after all his years on the police force. This girl with the open face and smooth brown hair could have been his own daughter; perhaps it was that sort of association that always troubled him.

She seemed unable to grasp what he had told her. '*Murdered?* But—*who*? Who would kill her?'

'There was another murder today with a very similar pattern. It appears to be a random killing.'

'But Mother has an alarm system. No one can get in without setting it off—it rings down at the police station.'

He nodded. 'She hadn't armed the system. It was turned off.'

She gave a little wail. 'How dumb. How could she have?' She stopped. 'Where is she? Can't I see her?'

'She—the body is at the morgue. You can see her, but you may prefer to wait till tomorrow when she's been taken to a mor—a funeral home?'

'Do my uncles and aunt know? And my brothers?'

'Your brothers were all reached. They're coming in—your aunt and uncles can tell you when they arrive. Your relatives have been trying to reach you all afternoon.'

'I was on campus.' Shakily, she stood up. 'I think . . . I'd like to call my Aunt Kay.' The surface sophistication had washed away. She was a girl in need of someone to take care of her.

'Let me ask you just a couple of things, then you can call her.' He felt cruel, deferring her phone call.

Obedient, she sat down again.

'Was there anyone you know of who felt animosity towards your mother? Anything happening in her life that we should know about?'

'Well, you see—' she looked away from him—'until

recently *I* felt animosity towards her. We were always fi—quarrelling, and I really didn't feel close to her at all. Then, suddenly, I'm not sure what happened exactly, but it sort of seemed to blow over. Lately we've had some good talks, and last night I was at the house till—oh, I don't know, eleven or so, talking to her about my plans.' She turned her face back to him. 'I'd decided on my major recently and I was pretty excited about it. History,' she added.

Pedersen glanced around the apartment. It had none of the earmarks of the usual college student housing. A long, low, black leather-covered sofa faced the fireplace; that in itself must have cost a small fortune, he observed. The bookshelves were not standards and brackets as he might have expected. Nor brick and board, certainly not that. A wall-sized walnut unit had been installed to house books and TV and, he would bet, behind some of those doors, a fancy stereo system and tape-deck. On the floor the Oriental carpet was so large that little of the hardwood floor was left revealed. Beyond, in a dining-room, stood a long walnut table flanked by matching chairs with seats upholstered in black leather and a long sideboard of some sort. Behind the pair of closed doors must lie a kitchen, at least one bedroom and perhaps a study as well. It was tidy, no clutter at all. This Suzanne must be a rare student. A recollection of his two children's college dorm rooms passed through his head; they bore no relation to this perfectly ordered apartment. Probably the girl's mother had a maid come in to clean weekly. Well, that family could afford it.

She had followed his eyes, her face blank. 'May I please call my aunt now?'

'There's nothing—no one else we should know about in connection with your mother?'

'No, I can't think . . . May I call now?'

'Yes. I'll wait till you get her.' As she began to dial, he asked one more question. 'Was your mother seeing a man? Or men?'

She put down the receiver. 'Just Ollie now and then—

Oliver Winter. He's an old family friend. Does he know? He'll be—' She left the sentence unfinished and redialled her number. 'Aunt Kay,' she said, and began to cry. 'Can you come over?' She nodded a couple of times. 'Yes. No, I'll be all right. Just come.'

She turned to Pedersen, rubbing at her face with a crumpled tissue from her skirt pocket. 'She was just on the way to my uncle's. She has to stop for a minute, then she'll come. She's been trying to find me. All afternoon.' She added, 'Oh, and Jed.'

Pedersen stared at her. 'And Jed?'

'I remembered while I was talking to Aunt Kay. Mother saw a man named Jed. It's Jedediah or something. He's younger, about fifteen years younger. I think she met him at a meeting of hospital benefactors. He works there.'

'Does he have a last name?'

'He must, mustn't he?' She hesitated. 'I'm not sure, I think it's Mason, but I'm not sure. It begins with M.'

'And she went places with him, saw him socially?'

'He sort of had a crush on her. Actually he'd be better for someone my age, but he hung around a lot. I'd run into him having drinks with her over there or they'd go out to dinner. I don't think there was anything going on. Maybe with Ollie, but not with him. It just flattered her to have a younger man so interested, at least that's what I think.'

'It won't hurt to talk to him. She may have said something to him.'

'You know,' she said, 'you don't have to wait. Aunt Kay'll be here any minute.'

'You'll be all right alone? Isn't there someone in the building you could call to come stay with you?'

'No. I'll be OK. You know, all sorts of questions keep popping into my mind and then out again. But I can wait to ask them. Oh. How was she—' she covered her mouth with her hand for a moment—'killed? You didn't say. Did you?'

'She was stabbed.'

'Was it . . . quick?'

'I imagine very quick.'

'She wasn't—' She couldn't say it.

'So far as we could see, she was undisturbed. Not raped. Of course we won't be sure till post-mortem results are in, but we think she wasn't touched.'

She relaxed slightly. 'That's good at least, isn't it?'

'Yes. It is. And I don't think she suffered.' He rose and stood hesitating. 'I guess I will be on my way then, if you're going to be all right. You'll feel better when your aunt gets here.'

She swallowed, her eyes brimming again. 'Thank you, Detective—'

'Pedersen. I'll be in touch with you again when you're feeling a little better.'

She walked to the door with him, polite to the end. This was a well-brought up girl. He nodded to her and heard the door close behind him.

Stanley came to the door.

'I can only stay a minute, Stan,' Kay said as she entered. 'I'm on my way to Sue's. That detective's told her.'

'It won't take long.' Stanley preceded her into the living-room.

Kay, pausing in the doorway, reacted as she always did in the face of the plum-coloured velvet sofas forming an L before the unused fireplace, the pair of beige-upholstered tub chairs facing the large glass-topped coffee table with its neatly aligned glossy magazines, its oversized cigarette lighter. 'You know, Stan,' she said, 'this place does look like the lounge off a board room. Why don't you have someone re-do it?' Immediately she was ashamed, both for saying such a thing at a time like this and for even noticing. Stan just needed a woman, poor guy. 'I'm sorry,' she said.

But his face grew grim. 'We are not here to discuss my living-room. It's a damn sight better than that ultra-modern pad of yours, I can tell you.'

'I am sorry, Stan. We're all edgy.' She seated herself in one of the tub chairs and changed the subject. 'Thank God Mother and Dad aren't here to know about all this.' As she said it, she felt the tug that mention of her mother always produced. Although she spoke of her familiarity, it was ever there, just as Ann had sensed. She had never known her mother, even for a day.

There was a silence. Stanley broke it. 'You're in a hurry, let's get on with it,' he said, more brusquely than he meant. 'The point is that there are certain things—family things and more recent ones—that we have to decide about. Ann didn't just die, she was—well, you know the papers'll dig up every last thing any of us has done in the past twenty years. We have to get together on this and decide what we tell them and what we don't.'

Roy spoke, his voice reasonable. 'You haven't done anything to be uneasy about.'

'You haven't done *anything*, Stan. Except in relation to your work,' Kay said. 'Isn't it enough that we have to—' unexpectedly, her voice broke—'cope with Ann's death, without all this other stuff? And you *haven't* done anything. You never do anything.'

Roy leaned towards her. 'Don't, Kay.'

'Well, I mean—he doesn't.'

'I didn't mean me,' Stan said drily. 'And I don't need an appraisal of my behaviour. You know what I'm talking about, both of you. There are just certain things we oughtn't to publish and we should get together on them.'

Roy smiled faintly. 'Get our stories straight, like a bunch of criminals?'

'I don't—' Stan began.

Roy waved a hand. 'I know. Just a bad attempt at humour. I, for one, shall be a model of brotherly caution and circumspection,' he said. He shrugged. 'Actually, I always am. No one's going to be investigating my personal affairs. And your business is doing well now, Stan—there's nothing there.'

Kay looked from one brother to the other, her face blank. 'Do you mean *me*?'

Stanley shook his head impatiently. 'I mean all of us. You know what family relationships are better left undiscussed. And I think we should all tread gently for a while, present a totally conventional façade.'

'You do mean me,' said Kay slowly.

'Now don't go away mad, Kay.' Stanley stood and walked over to her, attempting an awkward hug.

She pushed free of him. 'I'm not mad, I'm hurt. We don't all lead the same sorts of lives, but that doesn't mean—' She stopped. 'I can't—I have to go. Sue's waiting.'

'Can't one of us come with you?' Stanley asked.

'No, I'm fine.' She picked up her jacket.

'Just remember what I said. That's all I ask.' He and Roy walked with her to the door. 'You're sure—?'

'I'm *fine*,' she said. Looking at her face, Roy thought: She's not. She's showing her age. Kay doesn't handle strain well. He watched her leave, his eyes speculative.

CHAPTER 5

Freda Pedersen was avid for details. Over drinks, vermouth on ice for him, gin and tonic for her, Pedersen filled her in. He sat with his feet on the hassock of their lounge chair, comfortably established before their fireplace, which was still adorned with a large basket of dried flowers. Gradually he was beginning to feel regenerated. It had been a trying day.

'The first one,' he said, 'was a bag lady, name of Eugénie.' He discussed his cases with Freda. She hardly needed to be sworn to silence about them; for a woman with an enormous interest in people, Freda was remarkably silent about others' secrets. He told Freda about Eugénie.

She shivered. 'Was she asleep when she was killed?'

'I hope so. We don't know. It would seem so.'

Freda mused. 'A bag lady named Eugénie. She must have had imagination. And enterprise.'

'Apparently she did, she seems to have been the pet of the medical staff. But the second victim was a totally different matter, a rich woman who lives out in Galurna near the golf course. Big house tucked away on a private road. Mercedes in the garage, carpets you wade through, a fur-covered chaise in the bedroom. Even her college-age daughter is set up in a pad that would fill you with envy.'

'What makes you think the murders were done by the same person?

'The knives. Identical steak knives from Carson's, store stickers still on them.'

'Carson's? Maybe they'll remember who bought them.'

'I doubt it, but I plan to check. Surreptitiously. We're keeping the Carson name out of the papers, just mentioning that there were identifying stickers on the knives.'

'A bag lady,' Freda mused. She was intrigued. 'You know that client of mine who lives in Peter's Hotel on the mall? Maybe she'd know her just from walking around down there. She's no bag lady, but she lives on a shoestring.' Freda, whose activities included civic theatre and chronic course-taking, had added another to her list: she had become a lay counsellor with the community's Counselling Aid Centre. Lay counsellors had no professional qualifications but were specially trained to work with older people—lonely, marginal, troubled people. Freda, who had just finished her two-month training period, had taken on a client and was working under supervision, seeing her client once a week in the woman's apartment. It was at times disturbing work and often frustrating. 'But,' Freda had assured her husband, 'I'm learning a lot about *myself* from the workshops.' She grinned. 'I had no idea there was that much to learn.'

'Oh, I don't know,' Pedersen had said. 'I'd say there was quite a bit to learn.' He had returned her grin.

Now he said, 'You can't very well discuss what I've told you with your client. Once it's in the papers and Eugénie's identified by name you might mention it, but I doubt that your client will know anything. No one at the hospital, not even the social worker and one of the doctors who befriended her, was able to get anything out of her.'

'Eugénie's more interesting than Mrs—Koppleman, is that her name?'

'Certainly more mysterious.'

'Why do you suppose the two women were chosen as victims?'

He looked across at her with love, taking in the dark cap of her hair, her petiteness, her body, slender but strong. She teased him, calling him uxorious (she had been an English major in college and loved words), and it was true that around her he felt relaxed, at peace. Home was the best place on earth.

'That, Freda,' he said, rolling the glass with its dissolving ice cubes between his fingers, 'is the sixty-four dollar question.'

'Why *were* they chosen as victims? Why?' It was 8.0 a.m. and Pedersen was in his office with Tate. Pedersen admitted it to himself: he was confounded, more confused as to where to begin than with any case he'd handled. Because of the distance between the hospital and Ann Koppleman's house, the victims appeared not to have been casually chosen, but selected. The differences in the women, in their lives and economic positions, contradicted that assumption.

At least the initial findings in the post-mortems had given them something with which they could start. 'Now why in hell,' Pedersen repeated as he sat looking at the report, 'would anyone choose a bag lady to murder? Do you suppose he mistook her for a patient?'

'If he got close enough to stab her, he must have figured out that she was no ordinary patient. And if he was looking for a particular patient, he could see she wasn't it.' Tate rearranged his long, lean body in the chair and removed his wire-rimmed glasses to clean them.

'The PM set the time of death at between seven and ten. If it was on the early side, the room would still have had daylight. He could have seen what he was doing—and to whom.'

'The likelihood is that it was earlier.'

Pedersen nodded. 'Yes. Visiting hours, all sorts of people wandering the corridors, nurses not paying close attention. But was he looking for *this* woman, the bag lady? How could he know where she'd be? *She* had to check to see which room was empty. She couldn't know where she'd end up, how could he?'

'And the Koppleman murder happened sometime between midnight and three, the coroner thought on the earlier side. What did the murderer do in between? Did he have a third knife?'

'You think we're going to turn up another body?' Pedersen thrust his hand into his left jacket pocket, where he kept the green jade worry beads he had bought on his and Freda's trip to Greece.

'Maybe more than one.'

'Jesus, I hope not.'

'How about if I do what you said—cosy up to the street people?'

'Talk to them? Good idea. But change into jeans and another shirt. And get a little grime on you. Your hair looks pretty good for a street person, but maybe you can pass. Better than I would. You're younger, they might open up with you.'

Tate glanced down at himself. 'I can't do it in a corduroy jacket and flannel slacks, that's for sure. OK. I'll see what I can get.'

'I've got several places I want to hit this morning, among them Carson's. And I haven't really talked with Koppleman's family yet, I was so busy tracking down her daughter last night.'

Tate stood up and glanced at the post-mortem report. 'You know, Carl, it's interesting that both wounds were right to the heart. Done with expertise, isn't that what Rand said?'

'A doctor? A med student? Sounds pretty far-fetched even for Eugénie, who was right there at the hospital. But for Ann Koppleman? What would be the reason?'

'Well, in Eugénie's case, it sure as hell wasn't that they didn't want her cluttering up their nice neat hospital rooms.' Ronald Tate moved to the door, then hesitated. 'Could there be some point of contact between the two—a mission Koppleman was involved with that Eugénie used?'

'Could be. We can check it out, we have to check out everything she was involved in. She should be a cinch, compared with Eugénie.'

Tate raised his eyebrows. 'Compared with Eugénie, anyone would be a snap.'

Carson's opened at 10. The clerk in kitchenware called the buyer, uneasiness on her face. Pedersen had given no explanation for his interest, but she seemed intimidated by his size and air of authority.

She showed the buyer the knife. 'Didn't we discontinue this brand?'

The buyer examined the price sticker. 'Oh, this. Yes, we did. When we had that Odds and Ends sale two weeks ago I put out the last of these.' She turned to the detective. 'You want to know when it was bought, you say?' She frowned. 'It could have been brought then or earlier when we carried it as a regular part of our stock. All the knives had this same sticker, they all came from the same lot. What's the problem with it, sir?'

'No problem. I suppose there's no way of knowing who buys such things?'

She cast a pitying glance at him. 'How on earth could we know that? If it was bought at the sale and put on a charge—would it have been put on a charge, do you know?'

'I hardly think so,' said Pedersen.

'Then if it was a cash sale, there'd just be the register receipt with the department number. No way, sir, even if we went through every salescheck we ever had. Sorry we can't help you with your knife.'

My two knives, thought Pedersen. Or more? He left them looking after him, puzzled.

Pedersen had set up individual afternoon appointments for the members of Ann Koppleman's family, leaving his morning free. As he made his way from Carson's and down the outdoor mall, he detoured past the little park that had become a hangout for street people. A small statue marked it, a tribute to a local figure legendary in the town, who had dedicated himself to the welfare of others. Someone had knotted a tie around the statue's neck. Someone else had placed a bunch of flowers in a jam jar at its feet.

Passing the little cluster that populated the park, he caught sight of his partner's tall lean figure. Tate had moved in fast. Something had been done to his hair, it appeared slightly greasy, and he looked unshaven, probably from the application of grime Pedersen had suggested. He wore old jeans and a shirt that had seen better days and on his feet he wore a pair of scuffed sneakers that were both holey and dirty. Pedersen wondered where he had got them. He was lounging on a bench, whittling a stick with a pocket knife, apparently not in search of conversation. Pedersen did not catch his eye and suppressed a smile until he was past the group.

He doubled back and around the corner to the public library.

The library was beginning to be busy. Pedersen waited until the librarian at the circulation desk was free and then drew the photograph of Eugénie from his pocket, presenting his identification at the same time.

She was clearly startled. 'You want to know if I know her? What did she do?' She leaned forward to examine the photograph. 'Is she *dead*?'

'Yes, and we're trying to find next of kin. She's a street woman. Do you recall her being in here? Would you know anything about her?

'I'm not sure, she looks familiar. Did you try any of the other librarians?'

'Not yet. Just familiar? You never spoke with her?'

'I doubt it. Helen—Miss Perrine—has moved all the chairs to the back, behind the stacks. Sometimes they come in and sort of doze back there, get warm. There used to be a woman who slept in the lobby, but that's been stopped. Ask the others, maybe even Miss Perrine.'

None of the librarians placed Eugénie, yet several thought they had seen her. It wasn't until he spoke to the director, Helen Perrine, that he had results.

She was a handsome woman with an air of efficiency and good nature about her. 'Come on in my office,' she said, and closed the door behind them. 'We do get street people here. Most of them come in to get warm; they're chilled from the night. Some come to read or pass the time, I suppose. It must be a dull life.'

'I don't know.' Pedersen smiled. 'I think I'd find it pretty interesting figuring out where to get my next meal or bath or place to sleep that night.'

She laughed. 'That sort of interesting, yes. But not exactly—intellectually stimulating. Though,' she added sadly, 'most of those people are past caring much about that sort of thing. They seem reduced to a sort of primitive survival level. And of course some of them are terribly deteriorated. From drugs or just from living on the street. It's really heart-breaking.' She ducked her head in an odd little gesture. 'I'm one of those people who see a broken-down old derelict on a park bench and immediately think he was once somebody's baby boy. I suspect the truth is that many of them were once abused baby boys—or throwaways when they grew up. But I'm chattering. You wanted to know about Eugénie.'

Pedersen brightened. 'You knew her by name?'

'Yes. I make it my business to find out what I can about the regulars, the ones who come here all the time. She was an interesting woman, for one thing because she kept herself so well. She wasn't dirty and she had a sort of dignity about her.'

'Yes, several people have remarked on that. Did you learn anything about her?'

'She was a reader. Once I asked her about her schooling. She had been to college, she didn't say where. But I have the impression that she did tell me something about herself one day—what *was* it? You know, I see so many of them, especially older women. They seem to like the library. They can go into the rest-room and wash up uninterrupted. There's the public rest-room in the basement of the Kettle House building, of course, but it's always teeming with people. Mothers changing babies. Teenagers. Our rest-room is usually empty.'

'You can't remember what you learned about her?'

'Now what *was* it she told me? Or—you know—' she stood up—'you're going to have to let me mull, Detective. I'll come up with it if I don't try so hard. Give me your number.'

He handed her his card. 'You can leave a message or tell the switchboard to have me call you back. Try to remember.' He added, 'It's important.'

'Is there a reason, beyond finding next of kin, that you're so interested?'

'You haven't seen the papers today?'

'No. I never read them till evening.'

'Did you notice in last night's paper reference to a vagrant's being found murdered?'

'No, I guess it got past me. Oh.' She put her hand over her mouth. 'You mean Eugénie? She was *murdered*?'

'She was found stabbed in a hospital bed yesterday.'

'She was in the hospital?'

'She wasn't ill, she just camped there. Slept in an empty bed if she could find one. The hospital was upset that it came out that she was killed there. But some reporter got wind of it and played it up. I imagine the hospital is doing its best to keep local newspapers out of the patients' hands today. By the way, you wouldn't know her surname, would you?'

'No, she just said she was Eugénie. What a strange thing to have happened.' She shook her head. 'Strange.'

CHAPTER 6

The Mission seemed an unlikely stopping-off place for a woman who sought out an immaculate hospital room with private bath. Pedersen shelved the idea of that visit in favour of persuading Ron Tate to make it his next stop. Also, if possible, he wanted to interview Lewis Mawson—Dr Mawson, the man who so objected to Eugénie's incursions into hospital life.

A phone call produced the information that Dr Mawson would be free to see Detective Pedersen at any time within the hour. Pedersen headed towards Bay Cove Hospital.

Entering it again, he was struck by the difference in the ambiance from yesterday's visit. No nurses with alarm on their faces or administrators with apprehension on theirs. Today the brisk impersonality of the nursing staff had been re-established and none of the hospital higher-ups were apparent. He made his way to the second floor.

His first impression of Lewis Mawson was startling: the man looked Mephistophelian. The pointed beard, the ears set close to the head, the slightly tilted eyes reinforced the image. Although, come to think of it, maybe he merely looked Freudian. Psychiatrists went in for those pointed beards.

'Detective-Sergeant, is it?' Mawson rose from his chair and extended a hand. 'You're in charge of the investigation?' His tone made clear his disbelief that a mere sergeant could be in charge of anything.

'Yes, and another related case.'

'Oh, the Koppleman murder. I read that the *modus operandi* was the same in the two cases. I knew Mrs Koppleman slightly—a charming woman.'

'Ah.' Pedersen seated himself opposite the physician. 'I'm glad to hear that. Perhaps you would know whether any charity work might have brought the two women into contact. Did Mrs Koppleman serve in some capacity in the hospital itself?'

Mawson smiled faintly. 'A pink lady? No. She was a contributor, financially, I mean, to the hospital fund. She was on the premises occasionally. I would doubt that the two had met, although I suppose it's possible. What bearing would that have on their deaths?'

'Possibly none. We're just looking for a connection of some sort. The victims appear to have been chosen, not just randomly killed, so it seemed to us there might be some link. We've just begun to investigate, but so far we haven't come up with anything. This hospital affiliation of Mrs Koppleman's seems as likely as any.' He paused and then went on. 'Dr Mawson, we understand you were very much upset at Eugénie's invasion of the hospital premises. Resentful of it. More than some other physicians.'

Mawson picked up a pen and tapped his desk with it. 'I'm sure I have no idea where you got your information. I admit that I found it reprehensible, staff looking the other way as they did. It amused them—' his mouth curled—'they took her as some sort of pet. A hospital has a specific function. It is *not* housing vagrants.'

'Of course not,' said Pedersen mildly. 'I gather they were amused—at her cleverness in slipping past them and finding a room. And once she had used a room, it would have to be disinfected. I gather some of them figured she might as well stay the night. I understand she was not a dirty person.' At the other man's expression, he added, 'I understand your position, of course. There was no *particular* reason for your resentment?'

The other man gave a bark of laughter. 'Are you suggesting that I neatly knifed . . . Eugénie—' it was apparent that he minded referring to her in familiar terms—'because I, as you put it, resented her?'

'Hardly. Although there is one feature of the case that is interesting. The knifing was extremely precise, the sort of thing a physician—or a medical student—would be capable of doing. Have you any thoughts on that?'

Mawson looked at him for a long moment. 'None whatsoever. I must say, I don't understand your line of questioning.'

'It's spontaneous, my questioning. I'm just asking about what's on my mind. For example, it occurs to me that interns and residents are under a lot of pressure.'

'Interns are always under strain,' Mawson said coldly. 'They're learning to function without sleep, for one thing. But the teaching process is such that we weed out disturbed medical students long before they become interns. Occasionally one cracks under the pressure but that's rare, extremely rare. I know of no one in that condition at present.' He glanced at his watch. 'If you don't need me any longer, I have several things I have to attend to.'

Pedersen rose. 'Just one thing. Is there a Jedediah—Mason, I think is the surname, connected with the hospital?'

Mawson looked at him coldly. 'It's Martin. Jedediah Martin. He's our business manager. His office is on the main floor.'

'Thank you. Nothing further. You've been helpful. I probably won't have to bother you again.'

'Probably?' The man's eyebrows shot up. 'Well—' he stood—'I'm glad to have been of help. I think you should look elsewhere than on the hospital staff for your criminal, however.'

'I imagine so,' Pedersen said. He paused at the door. 'But

we do have to find someone who knew precisely how to strike a single blow direct to the heart.'

Jedediah Martin was available. A well-built man of medium height, casually dressed, he fixed his brown eyes on Pedersen as though he were the questioner.

Pedersen introduced himself. 'Mr Martin, we're speaking to everyone who was at all close to Mrs Koppleman. We understand you were friends.'

'Yes.' He continued to direct his gaze into Pedersen's eyes. 'What the hell happened? I could hardly believe it. I didn't know the family to call and say I was sorry—oh, I knew Suzanne a little, but I couldn't remember her last name. It isn't Koppleman.'

'No, she was the child of an earlier marriage. We aren't sure what happened, Mr Martin. There didn't appear to be a break-in. That's what I wanted to talk with you about. Did Mrs Koppleman ever say anything to you about being afraid or about anyone's having a grudge against her, anything like that?'

The man looked down at his hands, which lay flat on the desk. 'Never. Nothing like that. She was a lovely . . . easy person, a person no one could have hated.'

'Someone killed her.'

He lifted his hands and then dropped them to the desk again. 'It must have been someone who didn't know her.'

Pedersen stared at him for a moment. The man seemed genuinely upset. 'You and she were close friends? Or perhaps more?'

'No!' Martin stood up abruptly. 'I mean, we were friends, but that was all. Not that I wouldn't have liked it, but she . . . she . . . you know.' He sat down as suddenly as he had stood. 'I feel a little ill. Give me a minute.'

After a while he raised his head. 'Sorry. It just hit me again that she's gone. Really *gone*. To answer your question, we weren't lovers. Ann said she wasn't ready for anything of that sort, and she felt our age difference was an obstacle.

That was ridiculous. She was only fifty-one and as young a person as anyone I know. These days fourteen years don't matter. I told her, but she wouldn't listen.'

'What were you doing Tuesday night, Mr Martin?'

Martin looked affronted. 'I was—I was at a party, as a matter of fact. Do you want the details? Names?'

'Please.' He watched as Martin wrote them down. 'Knowing what you do of Mrs Koppleman,' he said, 'what comes to your mind as an explanation for what happened to her? Did she get along well with her family members?'

'I don't think she saw much of one brother, but she and her other brother were close and she once told me that her sister was one of her closest friends. I remember she laughed when she said it and then she said they didn't burden each other with intimacies and that was what made their relationship so good. It was an unusual view of friendship, that's why I remember it.'

'Let me ask you something else. You know about the murder here at the hospital yesterday. Do you know of any connection between the woman who was killed here and Mrs Koppleman?'

'No. I gather they were killed in the same way, same sort of weapon. I don't think that makes for a connection between *them*. I'd say the killer was just going around choosing victims at random. Their only connection would be that maniac.'

'Had you ever seen Eugénie—that's the woman's name—here in the hospital?'

'No. Some of the staff were laughing over her one day. To my knowledge, I never saw her. And I didn't consider her bedding down here a laughing matter.' His young face became severe.

Suddenly Pedersen was tired. It seemed days since he had eaten breakfast. He stood up. 'I think that's all for right now. Suzanne's last name is Ford, if you want to get in touch with her. Thank you for your help.'

The man walked to the door with him. Just as he reached

to open it he turned, his eyes filled with tears, and Pedersen saw how young and vulnerable he was. 'She was a lovely person, Detective,' he said.

CHAPTER 7

Pedersen stopped off at the hospital cafeteria for a bowl of navy bean soup and a roll, then turned his car in the direction of Stanley Potter's place of business. His appointment was for one.

He had scheduled the visits with family members separately, letting them know he needed to speak to each alone; to his surprise, no one objected. Speaking to them as a group the day before, he had noted that they reinforced each other in their reluctance to approach certain topics. Despite the fact that now they'd had time to talk together and concur on an approach to his questioning, he felt sure that, taken separately, he could persuade them towards openness.

Potter was a partner—somehow Pedersen had gathered when he phoned that he was a lesser member of the firm—in a computer software distribution firm. The building was located near the water in an area largely serving electronics manufacturers. The building was not imposing, a long rectangle painted grey with smart black trim. On the lawn before it an identifying sign handsomely lettered in black read COMPUSUPPLIERS POTTER, EGAN AND CARR. Landscaping gave the building its only character. Several flowering pears spread their shaggy umbrellas over a rich carpet of manzanita, which was broken by several clumps of rhododendron. Lantana in a calico of reds and oranges was set in boxes against the grey of the building and a basket of white azaleas hung to the left of the entrance door. The display was more relaxed than most institutional landscaping Pedersen had seen. He wondered if Egan or Carr had been responsible; somehow it didn't suggest the buttoned-down Potter he had met.

The receptionist had been alerted. 'Mr Potter is waiting for you.' She indicated his office.

Potter's desk was clear. 'Detective.' He half-rose.

'Mr Potter, how are you today?' Pedersen seated himself.

Potter let himself back into the chair behind his desk. 'In better shape. That was a terrible shock, finding Ann like that.'

'It must have been. It was nothing you could have anticipated, I gather.'

Potter looked at him as though he were mad. 'Anticipated! I should think not.' He clasped his hands as though he were about to wring them. 'Ann the victim of—who knows what? Was there a break-in after all?'

'No indications of one. Mr Potter.' Pedersen settled in his chair. 'Tell me about your sister.'

Potter seemed taken aback. 'Tell you about her? What sort of thing do you want to know?'

'Just anything that comes to mind. I need a picture of her, how she lived, what was important to her, whom she knew.'

Potter shifted in his chair. 'That's a big order. I'm not even sure I can do that.' He eyed the detective uneasily. 'I'll try. Ann was—well, a good woman. She worked for several charities and local organizations. Both financial help and time, she never skimped on time. She was a good mother. Sue's the only one of her children in town, but she has three sons away at school, living in other states. She . . .' He seemed to have run out of ideas. 'She was a good woman.' His eyes filled and he brushed his hand across them.

'What organizations?'

'Well, there was the University Garden Project, that was a special pet of hers. And—let me think. Marigold House, I think it's called. For women who are abused, I believe.'

'Did she do any mission work?'

'No, not that I know of. She had some connection with the hospital, but I think that was mostly financial. I don't think any affiliation with a mission. She might have sent a cheque now and then. You know—' he hesitated, as though the introduction of the topic might be inappropriate—'we came into some money recently. My father—he'd been sick for a long time. Parkinson's. Ann may have made some gifts from that money.' He looked around him. 'I put my inheritance into the business.'

'Ah. That must make you a very important partner.'

Potter looked vague. 'No more than anyone else. We've all invested in the business. We had a rather rough period lately, a competitor in the area seemed to be beating us out for major orders. It seemed a good time to put some money in the firm, and it seems to be working. We've picked up on advertising, have a couple more sales representatives—we're holding our own again.'

'The money was divided equally among the children? There are four?'

'Yes, four. We were five, but our sister died about ten years ago. Cancer.' A shadow crossed his face.

'So this second loss is harder, I imagine.'

Potter was still for a moment. Then he sighed. 'Harder, yes.' He returned to the original question. 'The money was divided equally among us. I imagine Ann's will now go to Sue and the boys.'

'Let's talk a little about the people in your sister's life. I understand there was a man, an Oliver Winter.'

'Oh, Ollie. We phoned him yesterday after we left you. He was quite distraught. He loved Ann.'

'Was the feeling reciprocated?'

'I don't know what Ann felt about him. I always thought she sort of kept him in reserve, in case she should want to marry again. That sounds ungenerous of me, but he'd been around for so long. From way before she married again.'

'Tell me about her marriages.'

'She was married to a professor, man named Ford.

Romance Languages. He was the father of the four kids. About twelve years ago he died suddenly from a heart attack. Ten years ago she remarried, a man named Ernest Koppleman. A lawyer.'

'Someone she had known before her first husband died?'

'There was nothing going on, if that's what you're getting at.'

'And that marriage, did it end in divorce?'

'No, Ernest died. Another heart attack. It's no wonder she hesitated to marry Ollie, she must have felt her husbands were—jinxed. She was very broken up over Ernest, maybe because she was going through it all over again.'

'You know, Mr Potter, that another woman was killed and it seems evident was killed by the same person?'

'I know.'

'Can you think of any way in which the two women could have met? We feel there might be some connection, but because of the differences in the way they lived, we can't figure out what it is. Did your sister take care of any vagrants, involve herself in anything like that?'

Potter looked at him for a long moment. 'She couldn't have,' he said, his voice uncertain.

'You don't sound too sure.'

'No. I'm sure. Ann cared about people, but . . . She—mightn't she have met this woman at the hospital where she was killed? She did go by there often. She wasn't an aide or whatever they call them, but she was interested. Gave them money.' He added, 'Especially after my sister's death.'

'We wondered about that. It doesn't sound too likely, not if she was there as benefactor and Eugénie there as suppliant. Eugénie is the woman's name, that's all we've been able to establish.'

'I saw that in the morning paper. They were appealing for information on her.'

'We asked them to do that. The trouble is that the people

who might know her probably don't read morning papers. Or evening ones.'

'Other street people?'

'That's right. We're banking on getting something from someone. She may have confided in someone, told them her last name or where she's from.'

'Didn't the doctors at the hospital know her? She—the paper said she stayed there, slept in empty rooms.'

'A couple of them talked with her. They didn't learn a lot. She had been married, but we haven't yet discovered who her husband is—or was. She's pretty much an unknown quantity, at least so far.'

Potter nodded. 'Maybe the killer was just striking at anyone.'

'He could have been, but the distance between the hospital and your sister's makes it unlikely. And your sister's house isn't easy to spot, he'd have to go looking. No, he seems to have chosen his victims, whether or not there was a connection. Let me just ask a couple more questions and I'll let you go. Tell me about Suzanne. Was her relationship with her mother a good one?'

'You don't think—'

'No, I don't think anything. How did they get on?'

'Oh, there was the usual mother–daughter nonsense from time to time, but I'd say fine. Fine. Suzanne is very broken up.'

'Any enemies your sister might have had?'

'I can't think of any. Really, I can't think of a one. This must have been someone who didn't know her.'

'Now. Just for the record, what were you doing night before last?'

Stanley Potter's face registered alarm. 'Why are you asking *me* that?'

Pedersen shrugged. 'I imagine I'll be asking everyone who knew your sister that question. It's nothing—' he smiled—'personal.'

'I was—what was I doing? This business has wiped out

everything else. Oh. I had dinner downtown at Blye's and then, let's see, I came back to the office for a little while and then I went home. Watched TV all evening. Oh, I ran out of cigarettes and went to the store. That's it.'

'Hadn't everyone here gone home by the time you returned?'

'Yes, that's why I came back. I did some paperwork and then took off.'

'Do you have a night watchman, someone to check people in and out of the building?'

'Yes, I signed in and out. My God, you don't think I killed Ann?'

'And your lunch date with her? When did you make that?'

'Oh, that's another thing. I called Ann when I got home. Set up the date to meet her at the Pelican. We go there sometimes for cioppino and we hadn't been in a while.'

'Was that usual, your having lunch together?'

'Not usual, I suppose, but we did it now and then. We were fond of each other,' he added defensively, as though someone had suggested otherwise.

'No special reason for the meeting?'

Stanley Potter looked puzzled. 'Special reason?'

'You didn't get together to discuss anything special?'

'Oh no. Actually, Ann said she wanted to talk to me about Sue's plans—Sue was there when I called. But nothing else.'

'I see.' Pedersen got up from his chair and turned to go. 'Nice office,' he remarked. It was. Grasscloth covered the walls, the chairs were comfortably upholstered, against one wall sat a couch with a coffee table before it and a pair of striking prints hanging above it.

Potter's face was wry. 'It must come off better than my living-room. My sister Kay tells me that reminds her of the lounge off the boardroom.' He laughed shortly.

Pedersen smiled in sympathy. 'You said yesterday you're a bachelor. Maybe it simply looks like a man's living-room.'

'Maybe,' said Stanley. 'I hope so.' He ushered Pedersen to the outer door of the office suite.

CHAPTER 8

Oliver Winter laid the newspaper down with an angry gesture. The story was the first he had seen and he resented it. Not only did it couple Ann with a street person, a bag lady no less, but it presented her in entirely false terms. She came across as an inconsequential society woman, pretty and idle. That wasn't Ann at all. Her substance, her—he struggled for the word—integrity were lacking in the description. He sighed. He supposed it was unavoidable, this sort of thing.

The thought that Ann was gone, irrevocably gone, swept over him again. At times lately he had felt something of a clown, the faithful ever-present suitor. He had felt she was, if the term didn't seem too ridiculous, toying with him, keeping him eternally on a string as though she might turn to him if nothing better came along.

And yet that wasn't Ann. She was honest, she had told him she didn't want to marry and that if he were willing to accept the friendship—she had called it friendship, he liked that—on her terms, she would continue to see him. Seeing him, she had conceded, included sleeping with him. He had accepted, but on some of those nights, waking with her warm body close to his, he had almost wept with longing, with his wish to make it forever.

Of course marriage was seldom forever these days, but he still thought in those terms: diamonds, matched wedding rings, bridal bouquets, honeymoons. He was probably too antediluvian to be believed, a real anachronism in these days of Significant Others, casual sex, two-career families, abortion, herpes and AIDS and the rest of it. Those things, the breakdown of tradition they represented, disturbed him but did not impinge on his life. And there was nothing casual about the sex with Ann. For one thing, they were mature people who knew their own minds, and beyond that, Ann had explained that she found intimacy outside of marriage difficult; he had always been sure she was, within the bounds of their relationship, perfectly faithful to him.

All that was now beside the point. He would never see Ann again, never be greeted at the door by her, never enter her bedroom, watch her brush her hair, see her shed her negligée, feel her come into his arms. He groaned aloud. For so many years—after her first husband had died and before she married Ernest and then during her marriage to Ernest—she had been a part of his life. Of course, during her second marriage he had been made to feel a little like a loyal family pet, but that was in part Ernest's doing. Ernest wasn't the most generous person in the world, despite his kindness to Ann's children. And there was that other matter that preceded the marriage, about which none of them ever spoke; some people would say Ernest had an—he wanted to think evil, but the word wouldn't come—a cavalier side to him.

He was restless. He had decided to stay away from the university today, unable to face the questions, the surreptitious glances, the pity of his colleagues, but now he wondered if that had been such a good idea. Perhaps being in his office—he taught no classes on that day—would have been distracting, even soothing. Too late for that. Tomorrow he'd pull himself together and return to campus.

For now, perhaps he could do something for Sue and her brothers. He had phoned Suzanne the evening before and learned they were all three coming in; he could suggest dinner.

He picked up the phone and set it down again, nausea gripping his gut. He sat at the desk, his head against his fist, for a few minutes until it passed. When it was over, his forehead was damp. He reached again for the telephone.

She answered on the first ring.

'Suzanne? It's Ollie. Have the boys come in yet?' They were men, of course, but he still thought of them as boys, remembering them roaring at high school football games, swanning about in tuxedos before their first proms, finally departing, one by one excited, for their respective colleges.

'We're driving out to the airport to meet them in a little while. They'll stay at Uncle Roy's and we'll be—' she hesitated for a moment and then went on calmly—'planning the service.' She sounded surprisingly steady.

'What about you, then? How about keeping an old admirer company at dinner? It'll be a real—' his voice quavered slightly as another wave of nausea hit him—'favour.'

She must have picked up on his need. 'I doubt that I can eat much of anything, but I'd love to come along. It'll have to be early, though, I'll want to be with my brothers later.'

'That's all right, we'll avoid the dinner crowd that way. How's five-thirty? We can go out on the wharf, eat beside the water. It may soothe us.'

'Oh, Ollie.' She sounded young. 'This is hard for you, too, isn't it? I know how you felt about Mother.'

He cleared his throat. 'It's a great loss,' he said, hearing the stiffness in his voice, but unable to avoid going on, 'for each of us.' He had always retreated into formality in moments of unendurable feeling. She knew him; she would understand.

She seemed to. 'It is,' she said with a brevity that suggested to him that she didn't trust herself to discuss it further. She changed the subject. 'I'm waiting for Detective Pedersen right now. He came by last night but he wants to ask me more questions. I'll be ready at five-thirty. I—' she hesitated—'I don't have to dress up or anything, do I?'

'Come exactly as you are. Sue, I want to tell you how *sorry* I am.'

Her voice thickened. 'I know. 'Bye, Ollie.' She hung up.

He sat looking at the receiver, wondering what he would do with himself for the time till then, three and a half hours away.

*

Suzanne Ford had barely composed herself before Detective Pedersen arrived.

She was upset by Oliver Winter's call. For some reason she did not understand, she had more family feeling for Ollie than for her uncles. Fond as her mother had been of Uncle Stan, Sue had always felt his mind was somewhere else when she spoke to him. And Uncle Roy's pleasantness was mechanical, as though the moment he left the room she was wiped from his mind. Ollie, on the other hand, for all his stiffness and coolness to others, listened to her and heard her.

'Miss Ford.' The detective was taller than she remembered, bigger. His face was lined and warm. 'Your aunt got here last night?' When he smiled, for no reason tears came into her eyes.

'See here, you're still pretty upset, you sit down.'

'No, I'm not,' she said between deep breaths. 'I'm not upset. It's just—' she laughed faintly—'that I'm upset.'

He laughed gently. 'Let's just sit for a minute. Your aunt did get here?'

'Yes. She was very nice to me. My brothers are coming, too. The twins and Jason.'

'Here? To the apartment?'

'No.' She was calmer now. 'I mean here to Bay Cove. They'll be at my Uncle Roy's.'

'Ah. I'll be dropping by there later. Perhaps I'll meet them.'

She smoothed her hair and adjusted her skirt. 'Well, Detective, what was it you wanted me to tell you?'

He gave a little smile as though something she had said amused him. 'Yes,' he said, 'let's get down to business. I'm trying to find out what your mother did with her time. Did she spend a lot of it on volunteer work? Did she shop a lot? Read? Listen to music? Have parties?'

'I beg your pardon?'

Pedersen smiled. 'Just tell me about your mother.'

'Will that help you to find her—the person who killed her?'

'It might. We might figure out where your mother met her killer, how he knew her. It might also help us to find some connection between your mother and the other woman who was killed by the same person, if there is a connection.'

'You're sure it was the same?'

'Pretty sure.'

'Well.' Suzanne tried to think. All she could remember was her mother standing in the hallway of her house, smiling, and then stepping forward to hug her hard as she left Tuesday night. 'She was a good person,' she said and then turned away, embarrassed. 'You know about her work with Marigold House?'

He nodded.

'And with the Garden Project?'

'Yes.'

'The Garden's apprentices come from all over the world to learn how to garden without all those awful toxic chemicals.'

'I gather. Sounds like a good place.'

'She typed at Marigold House. My mother could type.' She could hear the pride in her voice and her face grew warm.

'What else?'

'She worried about the street people.'

Pedersen sat forward. She had his full attention. 'How do you know?'

'Mostly by the way she acted around them. When we were down on the mall last week, I noticed it. She . . . *saw* little things I never even noticed. Once she looked as though she were going to cry. She was a very *feeling* person, Mother. You know,' she added after a pause, 'I went to see her this morning. At the funeral home—they call it a chapel.'

Pedersen waited.

'When Ernest died I was in Europe and by the time I came home it was all over, even the tears. And when my aunt died, I never saw her. Suddenly one day she just wasn't there.'

'Cancer?'

'Yes. For a while she was in her house in a room upstairs with the shades drawn and Mother taking care of her. I'd go along because I was littlest and Mother didn't like to leave me so much. Mother had just married Ernest and he was very nice about her being away all the time.' She was silent for a minute.

'Yes?' Pedersen said.

'I remember it all. My aunt just lay there, very quiet, and she would turn her head away when I came in. She couldn't eat, Mother would take trays up and carry them down again with a scared look on her face. And I remember when the ambulance came to take her to the hospital.'

He nodded.

'It's funny,' she went on. 'They let me see all that and then they said I was too young to go to the funeral. I suppose they thought I ought to be protected. My brothers were allowed to go.' The long-harboured resentment was still present in her voice, she knew. 'They weren't that much older.'

'You must have minded that.'

'I did. But later Ernest described the service to me. He was very sad, naturally. He said there were simply tons of roses—she adored roses—and all her friends were there. She had lots of friends. But I don't think it was right of them.'

'Shutting you out that way?'

'Yes. You need to say goodbye, even to see the—dead person, so it's real to you. Otherwise, it's sort of, I don't know, unfinished, I guess.'

'I think you're right. Today people have a better understanding of that sort of thing, they don't protect kids unnecessarily. I'm glad you saw your mother.'

She looked up at him, knowing the gratitude on her face was transparent.

'Did your stepfather adopt you?' Suzanne had the feeling he was asking merely to change the subject.

'Not legally. I didn't change my name or anything. But he was very good to me and my brothers. He was a sweet man. He died two years ago, but I thought Mother would . . . live a lot longer.

'It's hard on you, all these losses.'

'Well, my aunt was so long ago I don't feel it any more. And my father, too, I wasn't eight years old. But Ernest. And Mother . . .'

'You called your stepfather Ernest?'

'Yes, my real father was Daddy. I never felt right calling anyone else that.'

'I can understand that.'

'I remember him.' She looked as though she were about to cry. 'I'm an orphan, aren't I?'

'You have people that care about you, your aunt and uncles. And Mr Winter. What about Mr Winter?'

'What do you mean, what about him? Ollie's been around forever.'

'You're fond of him?'

'I am. He's like another uncle.'

'You see a lot of him?'

'Mother did. But in fact he just called. He said we'd find someplace quiet where we can be off by ourselves and have dinner tonight. He's grieving, too. He loved Mother.'

He nodded. 'Was he resentfull that she wouldn't marry him?'

She looked at him in surprise. 'Resentful? I wouldn't think so, I don't think he was pressing her. Disappointed, maybe.'

'And then disappointed again when your stepfather died?'

'Probably. But they spent lots of time together. He wouldn't have seen much more of her if they'd been married.'

She saw the question in his face. He said, 'I suppose that

living in the same house would have seemed like quite a bit more.'

'Oh—' she was surprised at the carelessness in her voice—'he stayed over often. I mean—' she caught his eye—'in the guest room, I suppose. Although it wouldn't have made any difference to me, to any of us, if it hadn't been the guest room. Mother had a right—' she stopped and smiled—'I was going to say had a right to any happiness she could get, but that's such a cliché.'

'You said you've seen your brothers.'

'Not yet. We're going to the airport to pick them up, my uncle and I. You know, I can't *believe* we're in the midst of planning a memorial service for Mother. She was the most alive person.'

'You were with her until a few hours before her death, you said. What time did you actually go home, can you remember?'

'It was about eleven-fifteen. We glanced at the news on TV and then turned it off in the middle and I left. Mother was looking tired, I guess I'd worn her out, chattering on about myself. Sometimes I'm such a *child.* Now I wish I'd given her a chance to talk. I can't remember her saying anything except "Yes" and "That's good" and "Wonderful, darling." She was a good listener and I was all full of talk about my major—I had a terrible time deciding on one—and about the boy who influenced me.' For a moment she felt brighter. 'He's in history and he makes it sound so *exciting*.'

'You must be glad at least that she knew.'

'Yes, she'd been worrying about me. I think she thought I might take a year off to decide and she didn't like that idea.' Suddenly fatigue caught up with her; she felt if she didn't lie down, she would be ill.

As though he sensed that, Pedersen rose. 'This is enough for now. You should try to lie down before you go out to the airport.'

She smiled. 'You must be a mind-reader, Detective.'

He returned the smile. 'It doesn't take a mind-reader.'

After she had walked with him to the entrance hall and closed the door behind him, she bolted it and put on the chain. She looked at her wristwatch and lay down on the couch. Fifteen minutes till Uncle Roy picked her up. As she closed her eyes she realized that she never locked and bolted the door in the daytime.

CHAPTER 9

Kay Brennan pulled one stocking taut and felt the run slide up her leg. 'Damn,' she said aloud, feeling the tears start in her eyes. It was her own stupid clumsiness, but today everything made her cry. Unsteadily she sat down, pressing her hands together to stop their shaking. After a few minutes she removed her shoes and slid the stocking down her leg, taking off the other as well. Glancing at the turn of her calf, she thought: I look good, I know I'm attractive, I can tell by the response in men's faces when they see me for the first time. Then why . . . She shook herself and went into the bedroom.

That detective was coming by. It wasn't important that her hose matched for him, but later, well, at dinner she must look her best.

Bob, her husband, was at the moment on the East Coast taking care, judging by his enthusiasm, of several kinds of business. Over the past three years she and he had moved into what might be called an Open Marriage. Actually, it wasn't much of a marriage at all; they hadn't slept together, despite her tentative caresses, her careful selection of filmy nightgowns and revealing undergarments, for nearly two years. She hated the whole arrangement. It had been Bob's idea; he said with all his travel, it was the only sensible approach.

Coming up with a pair of pantyhose in the right shade,

she shovelled the rest back and shut the dresser drawer. She must straighten those drawers. Irene, the woman who had cared for her after her mother's suicide, had been loving, although as an adult Kay had realized that it was affection born more of pity than maternal feelings, but she had also been indulgent. She had never taught her anything, how to care for her clothes or her house, how to cook, anything. She wondered if her mother would have been different, more helpful. If she was depressed, probably not, and she must have been depressed to have killed herself.

She experienced a familiar melancholy when she thought about her mother. It seemed unfair, all the others knowing her at least a little. Stan had been ten when she died and even Ann, at three, had vague recollections of her. Or thought she did. Only Kay had none. Her mother had not waited to get acquainted with her. She had never understood precisely why. She had tried to ask her father, but she was afraid of his cold grey eyes; besides, she found that all such efforts left her with the sense that it had been her birth that had precipitated the act. She felt the dull ache in her stomach beginning and shook herself free of that thought.

Her new hose on, she checked her face at her dressing-table mirror and went into the living-room to wait. The room was immaculate. Each morning a woman old enough to be her mother came in to clean. Mrs Espinosa had long since taken over complete care of the house: she decided what needed cleaning, she purchased cleaning supplies, she had her own key and went to work as soon as she arrived, even on the mornings when the mistress of the house could not drag herself out of bed. She must have observed things, with an arrangement as unorthodox as hers and Bob's, but she never said anything, nor so much as cast a critical eye in Kay's direction. Ruefully, Kay had come to recognize that Mrs Espinosa regarded the job as a job—her mind was on *her* problems, not Kay's. Another possible mother-substitute cancelled out.

As she seated herself and picked up a magazine, forcing herself to relax, she looked around her living-room. It was rather *Architectural Digest*, she decided. Stan had referred to her place as an ultra-modern pad and he hadn't been far off. But she liked the eccentrically-shaped coffee table, the post-modern pastels of the sofa cushions, the low deep furniture, the overall white look of the room and the strong colours of the two huge abstractions that punctuated the walls like exclamation marks. She had planned the room, it was something of her own, unlike so much else that made up her life. She smiled faintly as she looked around.

Settling herself against the pillows, she turned the pages of the magazine, but she could not settle her thoughts. What had happened to Ann was too much with her. Although the police had not let her into her sister's room, she had seen death, and a vivid image of Ann lying amid bloodstained sheets with rolled-back eyes and slightly protruding tongue stayed with her. The thought of Ann looking like that made her feel slightly ill. She and her sister had always maintained a special sort of intimacy, chatting about family affairs and impersonal matters and only occasionally touching on those things closest to them. She was aware of the loss in an unsettling way. Except for the unexpected moment, she was calm, self-possessed, not swamped by her grief. But it was there, nudging at her constantly. She could not escape it.

She wondered what her brothers were feeling. Roy in the last few years had increasingly distanced himself from her and Stan, she wasn't sure why, and Stan of course had been so full of the business and its vagaries that he had little left over for anything else. She wondered about Stan, not for the first time. So far as she knew, there hadn't been a woman for several years; she wondered if in fact he had someone, perhaps someone he considered unacceptable, and concealed the fact. But why should he? Neither she nor Roy would care. Unless it were Ann about whom he had been concerned.

As for Roy, she was touched each time she thought of him. Going to strangers that way—but of course recently he had developed considerably more caution—she was sure with the fear of AIDS he was not picking up any stray boy he might run into in a bar. And he must be happier than he had been in those days when he had made his try at heterosexuality. She shivered at the recollection of his ghastly marriage and the dogged battles over the child. Now that he had moved away from that, he was more relaxed in a superficial way and a lot easier to get along with. But he did not impress her as a happy man. She sighed. No question, Ann had been the best of the bunch.

She flipped over the page of the magazine and confronted an ad featuring a woman modelling a fur coat who resembled Ann. She studied the photograph, her eyes filling unexpectedly. Impatiently she turned the page and touched her eyes to check the tears. She wasn't going to be puffy-eyed from weeping when that detective arrived. Although, she reminded herself, he was probably used to that, doing the sort of work he did. Maybe he even expected it.

As she blindly turned another page, the doorbell rang. She dropped the magazine and, picking it up, knocked an ashtray off the coffee table. She had to pause to pull herself together. Then she picked up the ashtray and went to the door.

When she stood up to see him to the door, she realized she was exhausted. He couldn't have stayed an hour, yet she felt he had been with her, watching her with those canny eyes of his, silently noting every gesture, hearing the words she wasn't speaking, for hours. She couldn't recall his questions—he had been excessively interested in how Ann spent her time, but otherwise she could not remember a single particular thing he had asked. Further, she had found herself defending Ann, as though somehow Ann were responsible for her own death, a reaction on her part that she couldn't understand. But she had been discreet, she knew she had been discreet. She hadn't revealed anything untoward, any of the things about which Stanley was so worried. She knew she hadn't.

She supposed he would go on now to Roy; he had already spoken with Stanley and Suzanne. The problem with concealing information was that their stories might not precisely match; she wondered what, for example, Stanley had said about where he was the night of the murder. That was one question she remembered the detective asking of her: where was she the night Ann died? But how could she tell him where she was and what she was doing? This business of a routine inquiry was more complicated than she had imagined.

She checked the time. It was after four. She had until six before she would be picked up; she had set the time early because she knew, after her dinner engagement, she would want to spend the rest of the evening at Stan's or Roy's, seeing the boys and hearing what arrangements they had made. Now, however, she could lie down, try to calm herself.

But she was so restless she finally got up, went into the bathroom and undressed and soaked in a hot tub for a long time, trying to ease the edginess from her body. Then she re-did her make-up and changed into completely different clothing. Silly, after trying so hard to find just the right shade of hosiery to complement what she had been wearing. But the effort was worth it. When she examined herself in the full-length mirror, she recognized that she looked quite as usual, no effects of her harrowing hour with Detective Pedersen visible and none of the turmoil she was still feeling. She clasped on her little diamond-studded watch and glanced at it just as the doorbell rang.

Giving her curls a slight rumple, she turned and went to the door to let Lewis Mawson in, grateful that it was only at dinner-time and not after that they would be together.

CHAPTER 10

Ron Tate moved the newspaper that lay across his knee catching shavings from the stick he was whittling. 'Say,' he commented, glancing down at the paper in an offhand manner, 'did you read about the old woman who was killed?'

The man next to him was too strung out to answer. About him hung an odour so palpable Tate had to restrain himself from holding his breath. A young woman with a small child to whom she was feeding a bottle lifted her head. 'In the paper? Somebody you know?'

'Not me, I don't know her.' He eased a couple of inches away from the strung-out man. 'It says she holed up in the hospital at night.'

'She was one of us?' The woman looked interested. 'What's her name?'

'I don't know if it's here. I got this paper out of the basket over there, maybe the whole story's not here.' He bent over the column. 'Uh, her name's Eugénie. Pretty fancy. Know her?'

'With a hat. I know her.'

Two others moved closer. 'Shit, we all know her,' one of them said. 'You must be new in town.'

'Yeah,' Tate said, 'just came up from Lewistown. You know what they do there? They turn on the sprinklers at night. There's not a fucking place to sleep.' He wondered rather wistfully whether he came across as one of them.

Apparently he did. 'This Eugene person, she wasn't around too long,' one of them contributed. 'I talked to her one day.'

Tate restrained himself. 'Oh yeah? Wonder why somebody offed her.'

'She didn't sound like she knew anybody. She had some money, though. Bought me a hot dog.'

'No fooling? Maybe she was killed for the bread,' one of the men said.

'She didn't have *that* much. I remember she counted it out pretty careful.'

Tate held up the piece he was whittling.

'What's that going to be?' the woman asked. Her baby had fallen asleep over the bottle.

'Think I know?' Tate grinned at her agreeably. 'Well,' he said, returning to the original topic, 'if she wasn't offed for the bread, for what, then?'

'She knew something,' slurred the strung-out man suddenly.

Everyone turned to look at him.

'What'd she know?' asked one of the others. 'Where the fuckin' treasure was buried?' He laughed appreciatively at his humour.

The young woman responded. 'Maybe,' she said thoughtfully, 'she was a plant. Maybe she was working with the police.'

Tate, the plant *and* the police, avoided squirming.

'But she didn't seem like she was on anything,' the woman added. 'No, I don't think she was working with the narcs.'

'Who the hell knows? A narc can be anybody.' The man who spoke glanced around the group uneasily.

Tate turned to the spaced-out individual, who had retreated into his fog once more. 'What'd she know?' he asked.

The man looked at him vaguely. 'What'd who know?'

'The old lady. The one you said knew something.'

'Oh. What'd she know?' the man said, slight interest stirring in his face.

Tate glanced at the woman with the baby and shrugged.

'Why're you so interested?' she asked. 'You into murder mysteries?' She laughed merrily at her joke.

'No, I just figured, her today, maybe you or me tomorrow,' Tate replied.

She sobered at that. 'We don't sleep in any hospital.'

'You know,' the man for whom Eugénie had bought the

hot dog said, 'she told me something, too. I just remembered.'

The imagination of the group was caught momentarily. All heads turned towards him.

'She said she could have all the money she wanted. She said all she'd have to do is make a phone call.'

'Why didn't she?' asked the woman.

'I asked her that. She said, "Not yet" or "When I'm ready". Something like that. She sounded screwy to me. Weird.'

'Probably having delusions,' said the woman.

'Delusions?' the hot dog man said.

'Delusions, delusions,' one of the others answered impatiently. 'You know, when you imagine you see things. You hear voices.'

'No,' said the woman, 'that's hallucinations.'

'What the fuck are you, some kind of psychiatrist?' The man who spoke moved several feet from her.

She laughed. 'Screw you.'

Tate's curiosity got the best of him. 'I took psych in high school,' he confided.

It drew the response he hoped. 'Me, too,' she said. 'I thought I was going to be a psychologist.' She shook her head. 'No shit.'

'What happened?' he asked. He was touched by this young woman, holding her child with love, coping under who knew what circumstances.

'Oh, I ran away from home. My mother's old man was always coming on to me, and I figured before he raped me I'd better get out.' She glanced at the child and sighed. 'I liked school.'

Take looked away, afraid his feeling would show, and there was a brief silence as the group considered her remark.

'English? Did you even like English?' one of the younger men asked. By now there were eight in the group around Tate.

'Well—' she laughed—'I didn't like *English*, but I liked to read. I still go over to the library when she's—' she indicated the sleeping child—'behaving herself.'

'Nice and warm in there,' one of the older men commented. 'Got those chairs in the back.'

The subject of the bag lady had been left behind. Tate made one more attempt. 'I wonder who she'd have phoned,' he mused.

Several blank faces turned his way.

'Phoned?'

Tate found himself growing uncomfortable. 'The old lady that got herself killed.'

'Oh, *her*.' The speaker looked Tate over with more care than before, suspicion in his face. 'You're sure interested in her.'

Tate forced a laugh. 'Maybe I am a murder mystery buff,' he said, standing up and dumping newspaper and woodchips. 'I've got to take off. See if I can get some bread. I need a cup of coffee.'

'You shouldn't drink that shit,' the woman remonstrated. Then she added cheerfully, 'Good luck. See you.'

'Yeah, good luck,' offered another. 'That corner up near Kettle House where they slow down to hear the music is good. They might part with a couple of bucks.' He turned away.

Ronald Tate ambled away, aware that he had been wiped from their minds as though he had never been there.

CHAPTER 11

Closing her eyes for fifteen minutes had helped. As soon as she heard her uncle's step in the hall, Suzanne grabbed her bag and was out through the door.

'You had to do a lot of unlocking there,' he remarked. He bent to kiss her cheek. 'You all right, Sue?'

'Yes.' Her eyes filled. 'It's going to be so *good* to see my brothers.'

He opened the door of the Toyota for her. 'Great planning, their meeting in Chicago and coming the rest of the way together.'

She smiled. 'My brothers are smart.'

He laughed. 'You don't do too badly yourself.'

She relaxed as she seldom did with him. 'Seventeen should be clear at this hour.'

'Yes, we'll make it in twenty-five minutes.' He pulled out and headed towards the freeway.

'I've been thinking, Uncle Roy. Do you think it was someone she knew?'

He didn't answer for several minutes. They swung into Highway One and then cut off into Seventeen. 'Who would want to kill Ann? Who that knew her, I mean.'

'I can't imagine. She never did anything to hurt anyone. All I can think of is some abusive husband who felt she'd interfered in his marriage. Her Marigold House work. But she always said she had very little contact with the women, she spent her time there in the office. Besides, if some man were mad at Marigold House, he'd go after one of the directors.'

'So you're guessing that she was killed by someone who knew her?'

'I'm wondering. What do you think?'

'I think it's rather fruitless, this talk—it just upsets you. The police will find out what happened. We can't second-guess them, we just don't have enough information.'

'You think it upsets me to try to figure out what happened, but it upsets me more not to. You must think about it, too.'

'I try not to.'

'I—oh, damn!' She began to cry. 'It's such a mess!' She turned her head away and wordlessly studied the scenery for the rest of the drive. As they pulled up to the airport, she turned back to him. 'It's not *you*, Uncle Roy.'

'I know.' He reached over and patted her knee.

Suzanne spotted her brothers as soon as she entered the terminal. 'They're in!' She bounded across the open space between them, her handbag thumping against her body.

'Oh, Jay, Meri, El, it's so *good* to see you!' She had always been closest to Jason, the one nearest her in age. She hugged him hard now. 'Mother—it's so awful, isn't it?' She was laughing and crying at once. She blew her nose and tried to hug both the twins at once.

'Are you okay, Suzie?' Ellery asked. He sounded young and uncertain.

She smiled. 'I'm all right. Just behaving like a baby, as usual. What about you?' They picked up their bags and began to move towards the exit. 'Are you guys all right?'

'Better now,' Ellery said. 'Where's the car?'

In the car Suzanne crammed herself between Jason and Ellery and Meredith slid in up front with his uncle.

They drove for several minutes without speaking; then Meredith said over his shoulder, 'We talked a little about a service while we were on the plane.'

'Did you decide anything?' Suzanne asked.

'Small, we thought. With the . . . murder and all, we don't want to turn it into a circus.' He turned back to his uncle. 'Was there an obituary today?'

'Oh, Meri,' Suzanne said. 'It's terrible to be talking about obituaries for Mother.'

There was a little silence.

Roy spoke. 'Yes, it just said plans for a service were pending. We didn't say what day. That way we can let the people know who really cared about your mother and bypass the curiosity-seekers.'

'Will there be curiosity-seekers?' Suzanne asked.

'Of course there will.' Roy's voice took on a tinge of exasperation. 'This was a murder, for God's sake.'

The harshness of his voice silenced them all. After a while

Jason said, 'We thought chrysanthemums and autumn leaves. Would she have liked that?' He's trying not to talk about the murder, Suzanne thought.

'Yes,' she said. 'Those rust-coloured ones. And yellow. She liked colour.'

'It was easier,' Roy commented, 'with Jane. She loved roses so. Ann didn't have any special flower she liked.' He threw an uneasy glance at Meredith as though he realized he had said the wrong thing.

'She *did*,' Suzanne protested. 'She loved spring flowers, daffodils and narcissus and . . . tulips.' She began to cry. 'Oh, *damn* the flowers. I hate all this. Talking about what to do after someone's dead.'

No one said anything.

'Well, I do. When I die, I hope somebody cremates me in a hurry and doesn't say a word over me. It's gruesome.' She ducked her head, then looked up. 'There I go, acting like a baby again. I'm just so—upset.'

Ellery clumsily slid an arm around her. 'We all are, Sue. Somebody has to make arrangements. You don't have to be part of this if it's too much for you.'

'Of course it isn't!' She shook herself loose from his embrace. 'I'm just behaving foolishly. What about people to speak?'

'I thought we'd just let the minister say what has to be said,' Roy commented. 'He knew her. Unless you want to . . .'

'No.' She shook her head. 'No. I suppose that makes it less of a . . . circus.'

They were approaching Bay Cove. Roy sped towards the freeway into town. 'I thought so,' he said gently, as they rounded the last curve. 'Perhaps later, when this has all blown over, we can have a small private service in one of our homes, ask the people who knew her best to say something.'

'Yes,' Suzanne said. It seemed to her that would be worse, like reopening a wound, but she understood her uncle's reasoning. Or thought she did. They'd probably never have that second service.

'I told Ollie I'd have dinner with him tonight,' she said to change the subject. 'He sounded so forlorn.'

'Not with us?' Jason asked. He sounded hurt.

'I just couldn't say no, Jay. We'll eat early and I'll come by right afterwards. He sounded so sweet and . . . I don't know. You know how he can be, sort of severe and sarcastic, even? There was none of that when he called. He just sounded lonely.'

'He'd like to have married Mother,' Meredith said.

'Yes,' Ellery agreed. 'He's been hanging around ever since Dad died.'

'And since Ernest died,' Jason amended.

'Maybe she would have married him,' Suzanne volunteered. 'Maybe she just needed time to get over Ernest.'

Jason looked doubtful.

'Anyway, he does seem disturbed—well, of course he would, but more disturbed than I'd have expected. I thought for a minute last night that he was going to cry. *Ollie*. Can you imagine it, Jay?'

'Hard to,' Jason agreed, 'he's sort of a stick. Nice guy and all that, but not the sort you'd expect to give way to strong emotion.'

'Did you cry, Jay?' Suzanne asked.

Her brother looked around uncomfortably. 'Of course, I'm sure we all did. Not publicly, but . . .'

'I keep finding that when I'm in the middle of something altogether irrelevant to all this, suddenly I'm crying. I just don't seem to have any control, I can't tell when it'll—' Suddenly she interrupted herself. 'Oh, when you get to my place, let me out, Uncle Roy. I don't want to be at your house when that detective comes. I've had enough questions for one day.'

'Is he awful?' Ellery asked.

'No, he's nice, but enough is enough.' She looked fondly

at Jason. 'I feel so much better now you guys are in. I may even begin behaving like a human being.'

'You're enough of a human being for me just the way you are.' Jason squeezed her hand. 'See you tonight.'

The Toyota drew into the kerb. Ellery climbed out and released her. She hugged him and then stood watching as the car drove out of sight.

CHAPTER 12

Pedersen had learned to look at rooms, not just for what they told him of their owners but with an eye to description for a later session with Freda, whose passionate interest in houses had communicated itself to him. The Roy Potter house was a surprising one, unpretentious, undistinguished, not at all the house of a man who had recently come into a sizeable inheritance and had probably always been well provided for.

The living-room into which Pedersen was ushered held only some wicker armchairs, a slab with a corduroy-covered foam mattress, pine shelving and a rug made of rush squares. But as his eye moved around the room, Pedersen was startled. The works of art on the walls lifted the room out of the ordinary. One large painting done in strong shades of orange presented a woman's head with a compelling expression of deep mournfulness. Another, a huge, strongly drawn black and white print, violently distorted a spread-eagled figure. A third was a meticulously stated etching of men bound like sheaves of wheat; and a fourth, a delicate watercolour, pictured a vase of flowers; the flowers were wilted almost beyond recognition. There were more. Pedersen looked with interest at Roy Potter. He presented the same bland surface Pedersen had earlier met.

Suzanne's brothers had been waiting for Pedersen; that was apparent from the way they had arrayed themselves in the room. The 'boys', as they were called in the family, were Meredith, Ellery and Jason, three names not to be taken lightly. Pedersen suppressed a smile: Ann Koppleman had with all her children compensated for her plain Ann, unadorned even by an *e*.

At first glance, the boys—young men—were indistinguishable. Each had well-trimmed hair; each wore flannels and a blazer for the occasion; all gave the appearance of the prototypical well-bred young Eastern graduate students they were. Jason and Ellery, they explained, were in business programmes, Meredith in law school. As he talked with them, they began to emerge as individuals. Meredith and Ellery were not identical twins, nor were they much alike: Meredith was considered, thoughtful; Ellery more spontaneous. The youngest, Jason, seemed most visibly affected by his mother's death, although over all the young men hung an aura of depression.

'It's terrible for the boys and Suzie,' Roy offered. 'Frankly, I can't imagine who would do such a thing to *Ann*.' Pedersen looked up sharply at the stress on the name, but Roy had moved on. 'She was a giver, you know what I mean? She gave a lot. To everybody.' He shook his head.

Pedersen looked once more at the art on the walls. This mild-mannered man had chosen drawings and paintings stark with despair, hopelessness. He looked at the black and white print. And violence.

'You're a bachelor, Mr Potter?' Pedersen settled more firmly into the chair that had been offered him. It was remarkably comfortable for wicker.

'Yes, an ageing bachelor now. One early try at marriage. I'm afraid I've missed all my chances,' said Roy Potter agreeably. Hardly the usual bachelor, thought Pedersen, glancing at the sandalled feet, the hair curling into the nape.

'And your work?'

'I'm a bit of a dabbler. A dilettante. Actually, I had a rather good training in art history. I had a little gallery for a while. Now I'm working freelance with the curator of the

Bay Cove Art Museum. If he has something he thinks I'd do well, a show to hang, for instance, he calls me in. I'm working on one now. And I still collect and deal some.'

'You and your brother and sisters came into an inheritance recently, I understand.'

'Yes.' Potter's smile was unfriendly. 'You mean that obviates the necessity of my earning a living?'

'No, I didn't have that in mind. I—' Pedersen glanced at the boys—'I want to inquire into your sister's possessions. She wouldn't have had anything of value in the house—paintings, cash, jewellery—for which she could have been murdered?'

'She had a couple of good paintings. They were still there when I was at the house after her death. And jewellery. You must have checked that.'

'We did. Nothing appeared to be missing, but of course we haven't yet obtained an inventory. She didn't have a spectacular diamond or anything of that sort?'

'No, Liz has cornered the market there.' He smiled faintly. 'She has a bedroom safe behind a picture. Has that been opened?'

It took Pedersen a moment to register that the Liz to whom Potter referred was Elizabeth Taylor. 'The safe appeared to be untouched. It hasn't been opened yet. Did she keep a lot of cash on hand?'

'I wouldn't think so. My sister was big on investments. Every extra dollar went right into stocks and bonds.' His faint amusement came through.

Pedersen changed his tack. 'Can you think how she could have come in contact with the woman at the hospital who was killed the same evening?'

'*Was* she in contact with her?' Roy Potter stood and began to pace irritably. 'I don't understand the connection you make between the two. My sister had nothing to do with vagrants—street people, bag ladies. If she'd worked at a mission or something like that, I could see it. But she had nothing to do with any place like that. Why are you linking them?'

'*We* aren't, it's the weapon that does. I suppose you know nothing of her social life, the men she saw, for instance?'

'I'm sure,' Roy said, sitting down again, 'someone in the family has told you about Ollie.'

'Yes. I have yet to meet him, but I've heard about Mr Winter.'

'That's the sum total of it, I'm afraid.'

Pedersen looked at the three young men. 'You know of anyone?'

Meredith turned his palms up. 'We've been away since college, except for summers. Ernest was alive when we left.' He looked at the others. 'Right?' They nodded.

'You've made plans for a service for your mother?'

'Not yet.' Jason spoke up. 'Uncle Roy's going to help us. None of us has had much experience with—death.'

Pedersen was startled. 'You didn't return when your stepfather died?'

'I was in the midst of exams. Ellery and Meredith made it back in time for the funeral,' said Jason.

'And your father's death, and your aunt's. You must have experienced those.'

Jason looked uncomfortable. 'Dad, yes. And Aunt Jane—' he moved restlessly in his chair—'I'd forgotten that. I was still pretty young. But, I mean, we didn't have anything to do with arranging those funerals.'

Pedersen looked at him evenly for a moment. The young man turned his face away. 'Anyway, this is different,' he said.

'Different?'

He glared at Pedersen as though the answer were obvious. 'This is my *mother*.'

'Your father's death wasn't as upsetting?' The thought disturbed him.

'Well, yes, of course. It's just that we were young and Dad was away a lot of the time, working, travelling. We've had all these years with my mother. And she was *murdered*. That's different.' He looked as though he were about to cry.

They did seem like boys still dependent on their mother rather than like men about to enter the adult world of law and business, despite their having departed the family womb years before and gone to far states for college and graduate school. Pedersen's thoughts went to his own son. Was it illusion that made him see Matt as more independent? He was sure should Freda die—or he—Matt would be responding much as these young men were, and yet—somehow, he was convinced Matt would *manage*. Well, he sighed inwardly, they were managing, with the help of their uncle.

He rose. 'Who can supply us with an inventory of your sister's jewellery? And her safe?'

Roy Potter looked thoughtful. 'She was insured by Becker and Sons, all of us are. They'd know about the jewellery. And her accountant is Terence Randall. He's in the book.'

At the door, Potter turned his cool grey gaze on Pedersen. 'You understand we'd like this cleared up in a hurry. With no fuss.'

Or else, Pedersen thought. Ridiculous. The man was just expressing the usual concern for efficiency. But the feeling that he had been gently threatened did not leave him.

The message from the head librarian was waiting for him back at headquarters: *Please call Helen Perrine*. He returned the call; she had left the library for the day. No one answered at her home. Pedersen mentally shelved the matter and phoned to see if his partner had returned. As he put down the receiver, Tate walked in, his hair restored to its normal cleanliness, grime removed.

'*That* was interesting,' Tate said, seating himself. 'I had to acquire a whole new vocabulary.'

Pedersen laughed. 'You should be more profane, it wouldn't have been such an adjustment. Or is profane the right word?'

'As a matter of fact, the Lord's name is almost never taken in vain.'

'Did you find out anything?'

'A couple of things, neither of which tells us much. Eugénie "knew something" and a phone call she wasn't ready to make would have altered her economic situation.' He explained.

'Blackmail.'

'Sounds like that. I hung around that little Bennett Park for a while and picked that up. Then I tried down in front of Kettle House. No luck there. There are a couple of true psychotics that hang around Kettle House. One guy making those strange hand movements they do. How do you imagine he connects long enough even to eat, and where does he get the money?'

'Waxy hand motions and dull smiles.'

Tate threw him a puzzled glance.

'That's how psychologists describe schizophrenics.'

'At any rate,' Tate went on, 'then I moved down to the other end of the mall, in front of the bookstore. They weren't too easy with me and they were supremely uninterested in the death of an old lady. That crowd's younger, you know, mostly high school kids. I think they hang around swapping joints.'

'And other drugs.'

'Altogether, the day's work netted very little. Funny, at one point a couple I know walked by and looked right at me—I had a moment of panic, you can believe—but they never recognized me. Or registered that I was there, even.'

'We look right through street people half the time.'

'I wonder why. They're ordinary enough. There was a girl with a baby who seemed pretty together, not at all down, taking good care of the youngster. Though—' he looked past Pedersen out of the window—'some of the little kids on the mall are pretty forlorn. Barefoot, unwashed, trailing along or being ignored altogether. It makes you want to shake the parents.' He sighed. 'Undercover work is just not my bag.'

Pedersen laughed. 'I can see that. Let's work with what

you got. Did the person who told you Eugénie knew something say what she knew?'

'He was so strung out he couldn't put two sentences together. I don't think anything he said would be reliable, he just didn't connect.'

'Blackmail.' Pedersen was thoughtful. 'If Eugénie was blackmailing her murderer, does Ann Koppleman's death somehow tie in with that? Or did the killer just have a sheaf of knives and decide to do away with anybody who annoyed him that day?'

Tate rose and walked to the window. The gingko tree outside stirred slightly in an early evening breeze. 'Could Ann Koppleman have been blackmailing the same person?'

'Sort of ganging up on him?'

'But who? Who would Eugénie know that Ann Koppleman knew?'

'I suppose,' Pedersen said, tipping his chair back dangerously, 'the answer is to find out who Ann Koppleman knew. That's a lot easier than finding out who Eugénie knew. The only name I've come up with in a day of interviewing family is Oliver Winter, the devoted Ollie. And a man named Jed.'

'We could start with Ollie.'

'We'll have to.'

Pedersen let his chair fall back to its usual position. 'I'm going to check Helen Perrine again. Head librarian. Today while you were on the mall I visited Carson's, the library, the entire family one by one and Lewis Mawson. He's the doctor who didn't like Eugénie.'

'Some people put their time to good use.'

Pedersen grinned. 'Just what I was thinking.' He reached for the receiver.

This time he was successful. Helen Perrine, sounding breathless, answered.

'Miss Perrine, Detective Pedersen. I'm returning your call.'

'Oh. Yes. I remembered. Let me put down my things, I

just got in. Couldn't get my key to work and I had to run to catch the phone.'

When she returned she was calm. 'I remembered,' she announced.

'Yes?'

'It was a funny conversation. I didn't understand it, maybe that's why I remembered it. Eugénie was writing a letter— I'd better begin at the beginning. She came back to my office. My secretary had stepped out for a minute, so no one stopped her. She just appeared at my open door, knocked on the jamb and asked if I could lend her a pen and give her a sheet of paper and an envelope.'

'Was that usual, I mean for those people to borrow or ask for things?'

'No, but I'd spoken to her a couple of times earlier and I figure she suspected I had a soft spot where she was concerned. Anyway, I said yes and gave them to her and asked if she needed a stamp.'

'The library could go broke at that rate.'

She laughed. 'It's broke already. Besides, it was the first time anybody'd asked for anything. Then I asked her, as casually as I could, if it was an important letter. She smiled in a sort of—well, with someone else, I'd have said smug way and said, yes, it was going to be a surprise for someone.'

'That's all?'

'That's all. She took the stuff and went out. I peeked later and she was at a table, busily writing. Later she came in and returned the pen to my secretary. That was a couple of weeks ago, maybe a bit more. Come to think of it, I haven't seen her since. Does that help?'

'It may help quite a bit. Thank you. If you think of anything else, please call, even if it seems trivial to you.'

'Well,' he said, as he hung up. He repeated the conversation to Tate. 'That must have been some surprise,' he finished. 'It made someone go out and buy two knives the next day.'

CHAPTER 13

Pedersen came home exhausted. Freda, impatient to tell him her news, after one glance changed her mind. 'Why don't you just sit for a while, Carl?' she said. 'I'll get you a drink. Shall I put on some Billie Holliday?'

'Sounds good.' He accepted the vermouth. 'At what stage is dinner?'

'I'm in the middle. You take it easy. I'll yell when it's ready.' She bent to kiss him.

She restrained herself until they had eaten and then, carrying her coffee-cup into the living-room, she settled for a talk. The basket of dried flowers had been removed from the fireplace and a log blazed there. In Bay Cove fashion, Indian summer had ended abruptly during the night.

Pedersen sighed with pleasure. 'I feel about one thousand per cent better. Now let's have it.'

She laughed. 'Am I that obvious? Well,' she said, 'you won't believe it. Gertrude, my client, read about the Eugénie murder this morning and it turns out she knew her.'

'Knew her? Really *knew* her?'

'I suppose not *really*. By the way, Gertrude said it was all right for me to talk to you about this. It seems it was a sort of fluke. Gertrude sits in the lobby of Peter's Hotel sometimes. You know, it has that large window overlooking the mall and couches pulled up before it? Well, one day about three weeks ago she was sitting by herself there in the lobby, working up energy to go for a walk, when this woman stopped out front. It was obvious something was wrong, she looked ill. Gertrude had noticed her before, she sort of stood out from the other women that wander the mall. Most of them seem to be psychotic, Gertrude says, muttering to themselves and fishing in wastebaskets and shouting things at people.'

'That's because half of them, the young ones too, were let out of mental hospitals when the state made that sweep.' He grimaced with disgust. 'They were going into halfway houses. Non-existent halfway houses. So what happened?' She could see that the drink or dinner or her news had set him up; he appeared quite revived.

'As I said, she'd seen Eugénie before—she didn't know her name then—and she felt sorry for her when she saw her looking faint. So she went outside and invited her to come in for a minute and sit with her in the lobby.'

'She must be an unusual woman, your Gertrude.'

'She is. She's really remarkable in several ways. I wish I could tell you about her.' She paused. 'Anyway, after a few minutes Eugénie said she had dizzy spells from time to time, it was nothing. Gertrude was worried that she might be hungry, but she didn't know how to ask.'

'She'd have alienated her right off the bat. Eugénie was a proud woman. And?'

'You want more coffee? I can get the pot.'

'*Freda*, I understand that you know all about dramatic suspense from your years with civic theatre, but tell me what your client said.'

Freda laughed. 'All right, I'll get to the point. Gertrude said they began to talk. Gertrude's been seeing me because she's been so depressed since her divorce four years ago—she said it was OK for me to mention that when I told you all this—and they began to talk about marriage and husbands. Eugénie said her husband walked out on her. She told Gertrude it was just as well, they hadn't been all that happy, but it had been a shock to her all the same. She said in fact there had been several shocks connected with his leaving, but she didn't say that. Gertrude thought he must have had another woman or got custody of the children.'

'Did she say when she was divorced?'

'No. Gertrude asked, but Eugénie just shrugged off the question. Gertrude's seen her around the mall only the last couple of years, so she figured it was around then, two years ago.'

'The autopsy showed she was in her mid-fifties. There couldn't have been any young children to fight over.'

Freda leaned back, stretching her legs on the sofa. 'That fire looks wonderful. I'm glad it's cold again. So maybe it was another woman, it usually is. I only know what she told me.' She glanced towards the window. 'It gets dark so early now. A month ago I would have been working in the garden at this hour.'

'We're not even on Standard Time yet.' He sighed. 'We're getting the same stuff over and over on Eugénie. She must have had a certain body of information she didn't mind sharing with other people and that was it. Your client didn't by any chance learn her last name?'

'No, but she did say one other thing. Eugénie told her she'd grown up in this town. She commented on how much Bay Cove had changed. Then she laughed and said she guessed she'd changed, too.'

'That's interesting. You saw we had the papers publish her photograph today, maybe we'll get something. There must be someone who'd know her if she grew up here.'

'You'd think so. Unless she's so changed. But that photograph just showed her face, she didn't look like a bag lady, she looked like just anybody. Actually, from that picture, I'd say she was pretty good-looking.'

'She was pleasant-looking. All those people at the hospital wouldn't have fallen for her the way they did if she weren't. Although I think what they liked most was her gall—her gumption. I wonder what drew her to the hospital, it'd seem there'd have to be something.'

'Maybe she went there for emergency treatment and noticed empty beds. Or was taken there. She could have had a dizzy spell and fainted. Would she have had to show ID if she were being treated?'

'No, she'd have been treated as a transient. She certainly didn't have medical insurance.'

'Wouldn't doctors who treated her have spotted her when she showed up in a bed later?'

'From Emergency? How would they? They're always in such chaos there, I doubt that they recognize anybody later.'

'I guess not.'

'There's certainly some better way of establishing her identify than counting on Emergency to remember her. But her motive for being in the hospital—maybe it was those dizzy spells, she could have wanted to be where she could get help if she needed it.' He was talking more to himself than to her. 'It couldn't have been heart, the autopsy showed her to be a little undernourished, but otherwise she was OK.' She saw him catch the quizzical expression on her face and focus back on her.

'It was probably hunger,' Freda said. 'It's hard to believe people are actually hungry. And homeless. This is such a rich country.' She sighed. 'Last names are useful, aren't they?' After a moment she added, 'People living in cardboard boxes.'

He laughed. 'You lack coherence. But a social security number would be more useful. I'd know everything Eugénie did in the last ten years. Longer.'

'But she didn't have one?'

'Not that we've discovered. There wasn't a paper, a card, an identifying anything among the things in her bag. Only some money, sixty dollars.'

Freda's eyebrows shot up. 'That's quite a bit.'

'Yes, three twenties, as though she'd gotten them—been given them, stolen them—all at once.'

'Where do you go from here?'

'I have to think about that. Give us time, this is only Day Two. We'll get there.'

He believes it, too, she thought. Remarkable that he can have nothing, really nothing, and be confident that in the end he'll know. And he probably will, that's the thing.

*

With an exclamation, Pedersen woke. Freda, sleeping beside him, stirred slightly and thrust a vague hand in his direction. He had no sense of what had awakened him. Perhaps he had been mulling the case in his sleep.

He lay wide-eyed thinking of Eugénie, considering the information Freda had brought him about her. The fact that Eugénie had lived in the town all her life, yet had not been seen by the other street people until two years before suggested that something significant had happened prior to her appearance. Perhaps the break-up with her husband had occurred two years before, but wasn't it likely that it had happened earlier? She wouldn't have gone from being a wife and, presumably, a respectable homemaker to becoming a mall-dweller overnight. Wasn't the likelihood that the shocks she had described to Freda's client perhaps caused some sort of breakdown which then became the stepping-stone to her altered self? Dr Cohen had speculated on whether she had had a psychotic break.

Was it possible that two years ago she was in fact fresh out of some hospital psychiatric ward? And could that have been the reason for her attraction to hospitals? Why she found solace in a hospital bed—it was familiar?

That, he decided, is the direction we must take next. With the thought he relaxed. After a while he rolled over against Freda's warm body and settled into sleep.

CHAPTER 14

'Today,' Pedersen said as soon as Tate had seated himself, 'we start on hospitals. Hospitals and Ollie Winter are the order of the day.'

'Isn't that orders?'

Pedersen laughed. 'Order, orders, it's what we're going after. I woke up in the middle of the night with a realization.'

'A gestalt?'

Pedersen frowned with amusement. 'You're being very precise this morning.'

Tate smiled. 'I read some James last night, and I realize how imprecise we all are most of the time.' Tate, the son of a librarian, kept his reading tastes from most of the other men on the force.

'Fine. In my faltering, barely literate manner, let me outline a plan of action. But first, why do you think Eugénie chose to sleep in a hospital?'

'As opposed to what?'

'No, no, a *hospital*. Why would anyone go looking for a hospital as a place to sleep in?'

Tate considered. 'I suppose . . . let's see, if she'd had a good experience in a hospital, been treated and cured of something, she might think of it as a benign place.'

Pedersen slapped the desk. 'Exactly! It occurred to me last night that Eugénie may have been in hospital. As a patient, I mean. And considering the things we've learned about her, it could have been care after a breakdown. Yesterday Freda told me something that confirmed that Eugénie had a rough time after her divorce.' He told Tate Gertrude's story. 'Anyway, I think we should check the psychiatric wards of the local hospitals for a Eugénie. It's a distinctive enough name for it to be remembered, especially if she was there for any substantial period. I don't know what time to suggest. She appeared on the mall about two years ago, so it would have to be before that. What do you think, is it enough to go on?'

Tate looked doubtful. 'We can try, certainly. What about Lewistown?'

'Yes, that too. That's near enough that she could have been there. Let's try our two hospitals first. Then we can move on to small private places. There are only two I know of in town, but once we get into those, it could be anywhere.'

'Doesn't Lewistown have some small mental hospitals, too? They don't call them that, of course.'

'Yes. You might hit a couple of those. The good ones. Probably her husband footed the bill if she went off the deep end while she was still married to him. Meanwhile, I'll see if I can reach Oliver Winter and talk to him. How about if we knock off later and have lunch somewhere?'

'Minestrone at the Italian restaurant?'

'Sounds good. Let's set it for one. We should have made some headway by then.'

'Right.' Tate rose, smiling. 'You have Freda working on the case now?'

'That was her idea. But it was useful information, especially the part about Eugénie living here all her life. I can't believe someone won't recognize her.'

'No one's called in.'

'We'll keep after it. The *Banner*'ll cooperate if we ask them to run her picture again.' He slipped his left hand into his pocket and rolled the green jade worry beads between his fingers. 'It may take time.'

'All right. I'm on my way.' The door closed behind him.

Oliver Winter lived in a smart new condominium which overlooked the hills that flanked the town to the south-east. He met Pedersen at the door, meticulously dressed and still fragrant with after-shave, a straight-backed, grey-haired man of medium height who communicated a sense of unease despite his expensive clothing and the handsome furnishings which surrounded him.

He seated his visitor and offered coffee. Pedersen declined.

'I'm here—' Pendersen began.

'About Ann's death.' The man's face twisted suddenly, as though he had been visited by a momentary pang.

'Yes. You were apparently as close to her as family; in fact, when they describe you, you come across sounding *like* family.'

'I know the children,' Oliver Winter said.

'Tell me what you think of this. Have you any thought at all about who would murder Ann Koppleman?'

'Someone who broke into the house. Ann didn't have enemies.'

Pedersen liked the simplicity of the man's statements. 'None?' he asked.

'None.'

'You've known the family—how long?'

'About twenty years. We met through her first husband. We were both at the university.'

'And you courted her—' the old-fashioned phrase seemed in keeping with this austere, courteous figure—'after her husband's death.'

'Yes. Unsuccessfully.'

'And again after her second husband's death?'

'Yes.'

'With more success, I gather.'

'She didn't marry me. She might have, someday.'

'Mr Winter, just for the record, what were you doing Tuesday night, the night Ann was killed?'

The other man looked at him without expression. 'I was here, doing some work. Alone, there's no one to corroborate that. I wouldn't have killed Ann.'

'Did you speak to her at all that evening?'

'Yes.'

Winter's taciturnity was becoming wearing. 'Can you tell me about that?'

'I called late. Her daughter had been visiting and had gone. Our conversation was brief, we just spoke of plans for the next evening and I said goodbye.'

'She didn't suggest that anyone was with her at this time—what time exactly was it?'

'Eleven-thirty or so. No, she was alone.'

'You assume.'

'She said so.' A fleeting expression crossed his face, was it dismay? 'She said, "Oliver, I don't think I'll ever marry again. I do love it so when people go, even Sue, and I'm by myself again."'

'Wasn't that rather late for a phone call?'

'I called every night around that time. That is, unless—' He left the sentence incomplete. 'Ann never went to sleep before midnight.'

'You were about to say unless you were there?'

'Yes.'

'This must be difficult for you. Do you know of anyone named Eugénie?'

Winter looked puzzled. 'Eugénie? No—I, oh, that's the other woman who was killed in the same way that night?'

'Yes. Would you know of any connection between a . . . bag lady and your friend Mrs Koppleman?'

'No. And I've never run across the name, except for the French empress. I can't believe Ann had anything to do with a—' he spoke the words as though they were in another language, and with distaste—'bag lady.'

'Mrs Koppleman worked with troubled women. She worked at Marigold House and gave money to the hospital.'

'But those were troubled *young* women, women whose husbands abused them. And I don't think she had actual contact with them, she typed and gave the organization money.'

'They weren't all young. And if she was typing at Marigold House, she had some contact with them, that would be inescapable. But she wouldn't have met Eugénie there. It would have had to be somewhere else.'

Oliver Winter showed the first sign of irritability. 'That's nonsense. Ann didn't know her and that is that. The killer must just have happened on those two victims. I refuse to consider that Ann knew her.'

Pedersen changed the subject. 'What about the rest of the family? The brothers, the sister? You know them. Would any of them have had reason for attacking Ann?' He realized he had lapsed into the use of her first name. 'Mrs Koppleman.'

'They were like families always are. There were frictions, but nothing that would lead to murder. Ann and Stanley were fairly close, though I think on a fairly superficial level.

They didn't share deep values. And Roy, although he wasn't much younger, she treated like a little brother. She and her sister were close, I think they confided in each other. I suppose you've spoken to her?'

'Yes, I have. So there was nothing—jealousy, money problems—nothing that could have stirred one of them up?'

'Absolutely not. And the person would also have had to kill your Eugénie, wouldn't he?'

'He would.'

Winter stood up. 'I think you're barking up the wrong tree, Detective. You should be looking for some homicidal maniac, some psychopath. Why are you wasting time visiting me?'

Pedersen met his eyes. 'We have to eliminate those close to her first. And you were close to her.'

'Yes. Well, you've eliminated me, now you can get down to business.' He paused. 'I assume you have eliminated me?'

Pedersen stood up too. 'It's early to eliminate anyone. And we're looking for a psychopath, I assure you.'

Winter stared at him. 'You make it sound as though one of us—' He broke off. 'Will that do it? I have to meet my class at eleven.'

'Your field is—?'

'Economics.' His voice was cold, as though this question were the ultimate intrusion.

Funny guy, Pedersen thought as he made his way back to his car, a very funny guy.

The final search of Ann Koppleman's apartment turned up nothing new. The inventory of her jewellery matched the contents of her jewel case. The items stored in the wall safe were those the accountant had anticipated, along with several hundred dollars in cash and a will leaving Ann Koppleman's worldly goods to her four children to be shared equally. Finished, Pedersen gave a last look around the room opulent with satin and fur. It impressed him differently today than it had the first time he had seen it; today it did not suggest sybaritic self-indulgence but merely pleasure in comfort. The general image of Ann as a good woman must be sinking in.

Turning to go, he idly picked up a book from the bedside table where it lay face down, still gritty with grey powder. *Ironweed*. A gaunt male face brooded from the cover. He turned it over and read the blurb, conscious of mounting excitement. The novel's protagonist was a vagrant; the novel concerned the life of a nineteen-thirties hobo. Enlisting the help of the officer who had accompanied him, he located pen and paper, wrote a receipt which he left on the desk, and pocketed the book. Coincidence? The book was the first suggestion of a link between Ann and Eugénie; if not an actual link, the possible interest of one in the predicament of the other. Despite the lack of sound evidence, Pedersen was sure Ann had known Eugénie, it was a gut feeling. He smiled to himself. Better not make much of it with Tate until he had more; his rational partner would raise his hands in protest.

Back at headquarters, he put aside his impulse to begin the novel immediately and settled down to the paperwork that had accrued. Usually Tate disposed of that for him; paperwork was to Pedersen the least desirable aspect of the job while Tate executed it with admirable efficiency and no fuss at all.

Among the reports he found confirmation of Jedediah Martin's statement: he had arrived at the dinner-party at a little before seven, he and his hosts and their guests had spent the evening together and then gone on to a jazz club, staying until after two. Pedersen wondered how Martin could work if all his weekday evenings were like that.

In the midst of the work, he was called into the lieutenant's office for a report on progress.

Pedersen liked Lieutenant Harbison. He himself had long qualified to take the test for a lieutenancy, but as a senior officer who preferred work in the field, he had been liberated by the institution of longevity pay, which brought an almost equivalent salary to some senior men. People like Harbison were better suited than he to a desk and papers.

And Lieutenant Harbison, Pedersen had to admit, fitted the role in more ways than one. A tall, good-looking man, his face was tanned as though he had done nothing more demanding than spend the summer on the beaches and his eyes were strikingly blue with clear whites, the sort of eyes that by their colour and clarity inspired confidence. Pedersen gave a little inner sigh. In this man's presence, he always felt unnaturally large and awkward, conscious of the roughness of his own features, of his large hands and feet. But Harbison was a good man, efficient, thorough and completely aware of what his detectives were doing at any given time.

'Where are you with it?' Harbison asked, indicating a chair for Pedersen.

'Not much of anywhere yet, but I keep feeling like a cartoon strip character with electric light bulbs going off over my head.' He paused and shook his head. 'I think we'll get through the maze.'

Harbison tipped his head back and laughed. 'It is a maze all right, I can see that. Tell me some of what you've done.'

Pedersen outlined their activity of the past two days.

'Sounds good.' He looked down at the surface of his desk. 'You're not—coming down too heavily?'

'Harassing people? No, have there been complaints? Already?'

Harbison laughed. 'Don't worry. These seem to be sensitive souls. Stanley Potter. He's pretty well known in town.' He hesitated. 'And I just had another call. Did you visit a man named Winter this morning?'

Pedersen nodded. 'He's a close friend of the family. You have to ask questions.'

'I know. He called to berate us for time-wasting. Nothing

to worry about, but it's early to be getting irate phone calls. So—' he grinned—'keep on it. Do what you have to do, but none of this time-wasting.'

Pedersen returned the grin, but he was annoyed. The briefest of interviews and already Winter was carping. He had a feeling this case was not going to be solved overnight, neither of them was. Winter had better brace himself.

At quarter of one, he knocked off and put on his jacket to go and meet Tate.

'Nothing,' Tate said after they had seated themselves and ordered. 'Not one thing.'

'You checked Lewistown Hospital?'

'All of them. I even checked out the two local small hospitals. No one by the name of Eugénie. They went back several years in their files. Those little places don't have that many patients. But no one could recall her at the two bigger hospitals. Of course, nursing staff changes, doctors come and go; they could have had her there and not been aware of it.'

'Who did you talk to?'

'Mawson, among others. Head of Psychiatry. He'd certainly remember, given his antipathy for her.'

'He's been there for some time?'

'Fifteen years. He says he's aware of every patient that goes through his service.'

'I was *sure* . . . well, so much for bright notions. I suppose we should check the local small hospitals, the Lewistown ones and the rest. But I had a feeling . . .'

'Maybe she just figured out that there would be empty beds in a hospital. What other public institution—I mean one the public can freely enter—has beds? She'd need a credit card or money to get into a hotel.'

'She had money. Some.' He glumly attacked his minestrone. 'Mawson. You didn't think he was lying?'

'He didn't appear to be, but that would be a hard thing

to determine.' Tate ate silently for a moment. 'Is there anyone else, anyone she knew, who could have been there? Maybe she went to visit a friend regularly and noticed the empty beds then.'

'What about Ann Koppleman? I wonder if she had a hospitalization. That might be a link, maybe Eugénie encountered her there.'

'You want me to check whether they have a record of Koppleman's being there?'

'Yes, probably it won't take more than a phone call.' He helped himself to a second from the tureen. 'I was so sure . . .'

Tate laughed. 'You don't give up easily. I'll check right after lunch, but I'm not sure that's going to get us any place. After we find they met, if they did, where do we go from there?'

'I don't know. Maybe the killer really did pick his victims at random. I counted on a link between the two women giving us something, but you're probably right—where will we be then?'

They continued eating in silence. Then Pedersen said, 'I'm going to phone the family members and Winter, find out if any of them received a threatening letter or any sort of letter from a stranger in the past couple of weeks.'

'If it was a blackmail letter, you don't think they'd tell you?'

'Maybe it wasn't blackmail. Or maybe they didn't perceive it as blackmail. You have the statement of the guy on the mall that she could get money by writing—'

'Phoning.'

'Same difference. I have the statement from the head librarian that she was writing a letter that would surprise someone. It sounds as though she had information she thought someone would pay to keep hushed up, but we don't *know*.'

'You'll feel better if you try calling the family.'

Pedersen threw an amused glance his partner's way. 'Let's not worry about how I feel, what we have to worry about is what Bay Cove's going to feel if we don't nail that killer.'

CHAPTER 15

Kay was preparing a salad when the phone call came. For a moment she thought it was her husband, then the speaker said a few more words and she recognized Lew Mawson's voice. 'You sound funny. Are you all right?' she said.

'Let me close this door.' He returned. 'A detective was just here, inquiring whether their bag lady was a former patient of mine.'

'Why on earth are they interested in that?' She was conscious of her acute disappointment; for a minute there, she had been sure it was her husband.

'They think she had something to do with hospitals, that's why she chose one to sleep in.'

Where *was* he? Surely she should have heard something by now. She said, 'Couldn't they have assumed she was smart enough to know there'd always be an empty bed someplace in the building?'

'They could have. They didn't.'

She sighed and focused her interest on Lew. 'Did it upset you, having detectives around again? You told them you didn't have her as a patient, didn't you?'

'Of course I did. You know, Kay, maybe till this thing blows over—'

He had her full attention now. 'We shouldn't see each other?' She was aware of a rush of conflicting emotions. No more of Lew with his peculiar requests. No more of—but then she'd be alone. Until her husband came back, Lew was all she had. She shook her curls irritably. 'Not on your life, Lew. You dump me and I stay dumped. No resumption of our activities in the future.'

'Speaking of that. You didn't say anything to the detective when he interviewed you?'

She laughed, the sound shrill in her ears. 'You think I'm out of my mind? Aside from your reputation, I have my own to protect. I go along with your little—ways, but I don't boast about them.' She could hear the irascibility in her voice. The idea that Lew thought he could conveniently strike her off his list infuriated her. The things she had done with—and for—him. And lately he seemed to be changing, wanting to do things to *her*, things which genuinely frightened her . . . She had put up with all that, gone along with it, and he thought he could simply call and suggest that they not see each other until what he called 'this thing' blew over. Why, it might never blow over.

There was a silence on the other end of the line. Then, his voice constricted, Lewis said, 'Kay, it isn't *you*. You know how I feel about you. It's well, you know what it is. All I meant was that perhaps we could take it easy for a while, maybe see less of each other. Not stop altogether, nothing like that.'

'While you find some other woman to tie you up and tramp around on your chest with spike heels? Figuratively speaking, of course.'

'For *Christ's* sake, this is a hospital phone, Kay. Be careful what you say.' She could see him, sweat breaking out on his forehead the way it did when . . . He broke in on her thoughts. 'Let's have dinner and talk about this. I'd better not call you from the hospital again.'

'I can be discreet when I want to. I don't want to today.' God, why *didn't* she break it off? Was she as desperate as all this? What had happened to her lately? She sometimes felt she didn't know herself at all.

'All right, all right,' he said. 'You're angry. We'll talk about that, too. I have to get off the phone now and tonight's that dinner meeting. Christ—meetings! I'll see you tomorrow night at seven. Is that all right?'

'Tomorrow night we're going to discuss not seeing each other?'

'No! We'll talk about how we can see each other and remain—discreet, as you put it.'

Despite herself, she laughed. He was really a coward. 'I'll see you tomorrow night at seven, Lew.' She put the receiver down hard. Men were all alike, her husband, Lew, all of them. Interested only in their own welfare. She went back to her salad and, invigorated by her anger, tossed it vigorously and began to eat with relish.

Before she was done, she had a second call.

'Yes? Oh, Detective Pedersen. What—?'

He was inquiring whether she had received a letter, one from a stranger, a threatening letter, anything out of the ordinary.

'No, nothing like that. Why do you ask?'

He explained that Eugénie, the woman killed the same day as her sister, had written a letter shortly before her death.

'Oh. No, it wasn't to me. It wouldn't be to me.'

Had nothing at all come from a stranger? It might not have been a letter.

'No, I just said not, didn't I?'

After she had hung up and once more returned to her salad, she thought about his question. Had the detective asked only her or had he called Stan and Roy as well? It made her uneasy. In that unexpected way she had come to know, she felt again her sister's death as a real thing. Once again, she saw her sister's face with the rolled-back eyes, the lolling tongue.

This was no time for her husband to be away. To her surprise, she found herself longing for him as a sort of anchor, a consolation, a bit of normalcy (well, she laughed as tears tightened her throat, *comparative* normalcy) in this welter of strangeness and threat.

In a flood of unfamiliar feeling, she thought fiercely: What I really need right now is a mother to turn to. Why am I the only one who never had a mother, the *only* one? She was swept by a surge of envy that left her faint.

CHAPTER 16

The budget meeting had seemed interminable. Lewis Mawson rose and looked at his watch. He had an hour free, not enough time to leave the building for lunch. As he turned to go, someone touched his shoulder. 'Lew, how about a bite together? You didn't have time to eat before all this?'

'Fine.' Might as well, he had to eat. But a moment later he blamed himself for not having thought faster, claimed a commitment. He could have had Miss Roberts bring him a tray and had an hour of quiet to think. He struggled to recall the fellow's name.

They pushed their way out of the conference room, excusing themselves as they forced their way past others who had stopped to speak to friends, and strode down the corridor.

'Godawful, wasn't it?' the other man said. 'The salient points could have been put in a memo and sent to us. These meetings come oftener and mean less all the time.'

'Division chiefs tonight,' Mawson remarked. 'We *need* a second meeting today.' They approached the cafeteria. 'God, I loathe this place. Too bad we didn't have time to go out.'

'Just as well. As I left this morning, my wife said, "Jim, if you have steak at lunch, I'll leave you. I've got a big T-bone for dinner tonight." She knows my weakness for steak. I might be tempted if we went out.' He laughed in what was for Lewis Mawson a disgustingly jovial manner.

Anyway, his name was Jim. 'Anything new in your department?' He really didn't give a fuck, it was just something to say.

'Actually, we've been doing some vision experiments that

border on your field—well, on psychology, at least. You'd be interested.' He launched into a description on which Mawson found it impossible to keep his attention. Those damned detectives were unnerving him, that was the trouble.

They took their places on line, the stainless steel of counters and of the wall containing the microwave assaulting their eyes. 'This damn place glares so, it gives me a headache,' Mawson commented. Indeed, his temples were beginning to throb. 'God, look at this line.'

It was the busiest hour. The line inched along, those further back along the counter giving suggestive little shoves of their trays against the trays ahead. Mawson glared at the person behind him.

'That beef stew looks as though it would get us through the day,' Jim remarked in his expansive manner as they were finally served.

'It'll have to.' Mawson felt his spirits dip even further. Damn! Between Kay and the detective and discussing steak and beef stew with this ophthalmologist—why in God's name had he let himself get involved with the man?

He cut it as short as he could, hastening back to his office, head down and eyes on the yellow and green lines that ran along the floor, to keep from meeting any other glance and being waylaid.

Roberts was out to lunch. He checked his watch; she must have left early. He went into the inner office, closing the door, and sank into the chair behind the desk, head in hands. This whole business was too much for him. And what in Christ's name had gotten into Kay in the past day or so; she'd bristled with hostility. Maybe it was time to cut things short, not just because of this mess at the hospital, but in general. Yet he had a soft spot for her. She could be very elegant on his arm at a staff party and the sex had been good until lately.

He did have a raging headache. He rummaged in his desk for aspirin and finally came up with a bottle in which a single tablet rattled. Fuck! When Roberts got back he'd send her to the hospital pharmacy for more, if she didn't already have some on hand. He swallowed the one pill dry, tipping back his head and nearly gagging.

Pulling a folder towards him, he opened it preparatory to concentrating on something aside from his mental state, but before he had time, there was a tap at the door. It was Brown, the Adolescent Psychiatry man. He was new and still unsure.

'Yes?' Mawson hoped he looked as though he were in the midst of something uninterruptable. But he was discovering Jay Brown was not quick at picking up cues. Grimly Mawson reflected that he hoped the man was better at that sort of thing with the adolescents he treated.

'That kid, the one I spoke to you about yesterday?'

Mentally he rummaged for the case. Something seemed to be happening to his memory these days. He supposed it was because he was distracted by all those damned fool detectives charging into his office every twenty minutes. He dredged up a recollection. 'Yes. What about him?'

'I'm meeting his mother this afternoon and I just don't know how much pressure to put on her to have the kid institutionalized. He can go someplace good; they can afford it. And he'll never stay on the lithium on his own.'

Mawson sighed. Jesus, the man was a fool. Surely by now he could figure this out for himself. 'Tell her,' he said with exaggerated patience, 'the possible consequences. Scare her a little. But let *her* make the decision.'

Brown looked relieved. 'That confirms what I thought. I'll go after it right away. I was a little uneasy about putting pressure on her.'

'Pressure's the name of the game.' He wasn't talking about Brown's patient's mother.

'I guess so. You look a little beat yourself. Are they bugging you over the woman who was murdered?'

Mawson straightened in his chair. How could the man know that? 'Why should they be?' he asked icily.

'Oh, I heard the police had been around. You're not the only one, if that helps.'

'Who else are they talking to?' He couldn't keep the urgency out of his voice.

'Oh, Jerry Cohen, Rod MacMillan, some of the nurses, I've heard.'

Mawson stood up abruptly. 'Jay, I have some work I have to get to.' He forced himself to be civil. 'You'll do fine with your client's mother.'

Brown moved to go and then turned back. 'I hear you didn't like Eugénie—that's her name. You wanted her out of here.'

'That's nonsense!' Mawson's grip on himself almost slipped. 'A hospital's no place for vagrants to be bedding down, but I had nothing against the woman personally.' Why the hell was he explaining? 'Really, Jay, I must—' He had never been so glad to see anyone leave his office.

After Brown had gone, he sank into his chair again. He wished to hell he had never let anyone know how he felt about Eugénie. For all he could tell, the whole damned hospital was abuzz with his dislike of her. He wouldn't give a shit if only Rod MacMillan didn't know what he knew about him and Eugénie. And in a weak moment he'd had to go and tell Kay all about it. Fuck it all, no wonder he was a nervous wreck.

He leaned back and massaged the stiffness in the nape of his neck. As he sat there, he heard Miss Roberts enter the outside office and pull her desk drawer out, he assumed to put her bag away.

He went out into her office. 'You went to lunch early.' He knew he sounded accusing.

She seemed unruffled. 'The calls were taken by the switchboard,' she said blandly. 'I thought you'd prefer to have me out while you were away.'

'Well, you might let me know your plans. Do you have aspirin?'

'You mean you want some aspirin?'

'That's what I said, didn't I?'

'Yes, I have some.' She opened a desk drawer. He could see that it was in perfect order. The file clerk mentality, that was Roberts.

'Can you get me a cup of coffee before that patient is brought in?'

'Of course.' She removed her bag from the desk drawer and departed. The switch of her skirt suggested that she would not be cooperative the rest of that day.

He sighed and went back into his office. He wondered if he'd make it through the evening meeting.

CHAPTER 17

At work in the museum, Roy Potter reflected that he had begun to find the boys wearing. Fond as he was of them, it was impossible not to note how unformed they were, how immature. He was working on a show that got him out of the house frequently, but when he returned they were there, three good-looking lumps. The plans for the service were complete, notes had been sent to out-of-town friends who might want to attend, flowers had been ordered and refreshments arranged for—actually there was nothing left that needed doing.

Remembering back to his own days as a graduate student, he recalled having books to read, papers to write. None of these three young men seemed burdened by such responsibilities. He had asked Meredith. The boy—man—had looked at him in a puzzled way and said, 'I'm pretty distracted right now.' It was a legitimate out, but . . . Perhaps he had been a grind and not known it. At any rate, they were hard to fathom. The glancing thought crossed his mind that perhaps they knew about him. Could that account for their unresponsiveness—apprehension? For God's sake, they didn't think . . .? He shook off the thought, but he was troubled.

He had brought along his colour samples to the museum for final consideration. The background would be important to this exhibit; the painter had been influenced by the Japanese, and his works, a softly coloured single flower in a vase, a bird drooping against a snowbank, stark yet tender works, needed precisely the right backdrop. He thought the muted grey-green would do it. For a few minutes he lost himself in contemplation of the show, forgetting the ugly death of his sister, the irritating presence of the boys, the abstinence he had imposed on himself while the case was being investigated. He walked back to the museum director's office. It was, as always, cluttered with leftovers from former exhibits: rolled posters, boxes of museum postcards, not-yet-claimed paintings from former shows. In the midst of this chaos, John Hobson, the director, sat at his huge table, intently examining slides.

'Someone trying to coax you to do a show?' Roy asked.

'Yes. He's good. Look.' He held out the little hand slide projector.

Roy pressed the button that lighted it. 'He is good.' He returned the projector. 'You have a minute?'

Hobson put down the slides. 'Sure. Have you made a decision?'

'I think this green.' Roy bent over the table to show him the colour chip. 'I used posterboard for this colour to see the effect of a larger area. It works well with the paintings.'

Hobson considered. 'It's good. More interesting than the putty colour you were thinking about, but subtle. Good. Let's go with it.'

Roy experienced the stab of pleasure that accompanied approval from someone in authority. He supposed it dated from his relationship with his father. God knows, that man had never given him any encouragement. His sisters complained that they didn't understand him, didn't know what moved him. Well, this did.

As he started out of the office, the phone rang. 'Roy,' Hobson called after him, 'this is for you.'

'For me? Must be one of my nephews, no one else knows I'm here. Don't go out, it won't be anything that personal.'

The caller was not a nephew but Detective Pedersen. Roy frowned. 'Yes. What can I do for you?'

Pedersen told him.

'No, I haven't received anything like that. Nothing threatening. Nothing from a stranger, except some junk mail, of course, and pleas for money. Have you found something?'

The detective said no, they were just checking, the woman who had been murdered the same day as his sister had written someone a letter.

'Well, it couldn't be *me*. I've never seen the woman in my life.' He hesitated. 'Could she have written my sister Ann?'

Hobson had risen and strolled into his secretary's office.

The detective explained that nothing had been found among her papers.

'Sorry, then, I'm afraid I can't help you. How'd you get my number here, anyway?'

The boys had given it to him. Irritation again swept over Roy. 'Fine. Glad you could get me. Sorry I can't help.' He hung up and Hobson ambled back in. 'That was the police.'

Hobson looked at him with curiosity. 'This must be a terrible time for you. Have they located the man who broke in?'

'They keep saying no one did break in. The police work in mysterious ways all right.'

'I imagine. You're sure you're up to working so soon?'

'It couldn't be better timed, I'd go mad hanging around my house with my three depressed nephews. I'll get back to work now. I thought the large bird right inside the entrance, by itself. What do you think?'

'Fine. I leave it to you. However you see it is OK. This is your show, Roy.'

CHAPTER 18

Pedersen had reached Stanley Potter at work and asked his question about the letter with no greater success than he had with his sister and brother. Suzanne was not at home, but Pedersen was sure that she, of all of them, would have let him know had anything extraordinary come her way. The effort had produced nothing but further frustration.

He was sitting at his desk playing with his worry beads when Tate came in. The hospital had refused to give information by telephone and he had just returned from another trip across town. It had added up to a huge zero. Well, not quite.

'What,' he said, seating himself with a self-satisfied air, 'did you say the dead sister's name was?'

'The dead sister? What are you talking about?'

'Remember the member of the Potter family that died of cancer, the sister? What did you say her name was?'

'I didn't, I never knew it. Oh, wait. Aunt Jane, that's what one of the Potter boys called her.'

'Yes, well, she didn't die of cancer.'

'What did she die of?'

'Ann Koppleman was never a patient at any of the major hospitals, but Jane Potter was.'

'We knew that. That's years ago.'

'Yes, but she didn't have cancer. She was in a psychiatric ward and she committed suicide.'

'Suicide?'

'Yes. She was admitted to Bay Cove Hospital for profound depression, stayed the maximum ten days and was transferred to a private psychiatric facility.' He consulted his notes. 'Fernwood. In Lewistown. A few months later she signed herself out. Apparently she had signed herself in, so that was all right. A couple of weeks later the hospital learned she had been a suicide. That was all they knew at Bay Cove.'

'Interesting. How did you happen to ask?'

'I was asking about Ann Koppleman and I mentioned that her name had been Ford and before that Potter. They checked all three and came up with a Jane Potter. I was sure that was her name, you must have mentioned it, so I got all the information they'd give me. Someone had scribbled in a note at the end of her file: "Suicide." Must have heard through the other hospital. The Admission person said she shouldn't, as she put it, share such information but in the circumstances . . .' He laughed.

'So much for confidentiality. And all the friends of the family assumed she had died after a bout with cancer. Amazing. They must have kept the suicide out of the papers. It does cast a different light on things. On *them.*'

'Yes. We should go out to Fernwood and see if we can fill things in.'

'We should. First thing tomorrow. Right now I have to read a novel.'

'A novel?'

'*Ironweed.* I found it on Ann Koppleman's bedside table.' He explained.

'Sounds like a pleasant way to spend the rest of the afternoon. Sure you wouldn't rather have me read it?'

Pedersen grinned. 'I'm sure. I'm curious about this book.'

Ironweed was a remarkable book. The tale of an ex-ballplayer, drunk, sometime gravedigger, roaming the streets of Albany, revisiting the scenes of past pleasure and pain, gripped him, showed him the tragedy of the alienation of this group as it had never been shown him. He wondered how far into it Ann had read by the time of her death, whether she had felt repugnance or sympathy. Or both. He had. Even empathy.

There could have been any number of reasons for her reading the book aside from a possible connection with

Eugénie. Perhaps she was merely a naturally intellectual, inquisitive woman. Perhaps she belonged to a book discussion group. Perhaps she had seen the film. Those were things he could check. But despite what reason told him, a little worm of excitement was wriggling. It was a difficult book, demanding and upsetting. How much motivation would it take to keep a person reading? The marker in the novel suggested that she was well past the middle, but the marker could have been misplaced in the fingerprinting.

He got up heavily from his chair. He had spent the rest of the afternoon and the evening reading *Ironweed* and he ached from the sitting and from the intensity of his concentration. He stretched, yawned and made his way into the darkened room where Freda, having finally given up on him, was already asleep.

CHAPTER 19

Everything about Fernwood denied its intent: the treatment of mental illness. The soft roundness of the foliage, the low building, white clapboard with brick chimneys, the casement windows, all cried out its normalcy. Surely no one could remain depressed or out of touch for long in such a benign environment, it said. Only the locked front door told them the patients needed protection from themselves.

The two men were admitted and moved past bright chintzes and bowls of fresh flowers to a pleasant office lighted by several windows. The rather severe-looking young woman who rose to greet them was presumably an Administrative Assistant; she seemed disturbed by their request that they see the director, as though her major function were to protect her against such invaders. 'I'm sure I can help you, sir,' she said with great confidence, waving them to chairs. 'She's terribly busy right now, not seeing anyone.'

Pedersen was polite as he demurred. He explained. 'The

director is the only person with the authority to give us the information we need.'

'If it's just information—'

Pedersen broke in gently. 'Will you let the director know we're here?' She studied his face for a moment and reluctantly gave up. 'I'll *see*,' she said, not totally succumbing. 'She may be tied up or—' At Pedersen's expression, she departed hastily.

'Nice place,' Tate said, looking at the green beyond the windows.

'It is. Sobering when you see what money can buy.'

The woman who entered the room and firmly closed the door on her assistant was a surprise: blonde, startlingly blonde, another Marilyn Monroe, with white skin and almost white hair wrapped smoothly around her head. She had a sensible air that belied her sensational good looks. They rose to greet her.

'How do you do. We'll stay in here, there are people in my office.' She seated herself at the Administrative Assistant's desk.

So she had been busy. 'We're inquiring,' Pedersen said, after introductions had been made, 'into a former patient of yours, a Jane Potter. She left here some nine or ten years ago. We realize records are confidential, but we'd like what information you can give us.'

'I see,' she said. 'You realize that will be very little. What is it you want to know about her?'

'First, when did she come to you and in what shape was she?'

'And second?'

'The circumstances of her leaving and her condition then.'

'You're not inquiring into the course of treatment, the therapy, the reasons she was here?'

'As much of that as you're free to tell me. I understand your position.'

'I'll have to pull her records. We have everything on computer now, even our old records, so it won't take long.

I'll have a printout in a minute. Would you care to look around the place while you wait?'

They strolled through the rooms to which she had directed them. In the dining-room bright blue tablecloths were set off by bowls of chrysanthemums. The library was amply stocked; comfortable chairs were scattered through the room.

Tate pulled a book from a shelf. 'Right up to the minute. I've been wanting to read this biography.' Reluctantly he returned it to the bookcase.

On the far side of the building the garden with paths marked by clumps of autumn flowers was walled by stone, but the walls were covered with tumbling white solanum, small-blossomed potato vine. Here and there a patient strolled, accompanied by an attendant. No white coats were in evidence.

Pedersen grunted. 'This is obviously the place to be mentally ill.'

'If you can afford it.'

'Yes, it must cost. Wonder which of them paid her bill.'

When they returned to the office, the director was ready for them. 'Jane Potter was transferred here from Bay Cove Hospital—' she gave them the date—'as a voluntary admission. You've spoken with Bay Cove?'

'Yes,' Pedersen said.

'Then you know about the suicide attempt before she was admitted there.'

Tate nodded. 'Yes,' Pedersen lied.

'Her treatment went well, she steadily improved, and we were—actually, I wasn't here at that time, you realize?—we were discussing home visits at the time she decided to sign herself out. It was against our judgement that she be discharged without any family present to see her on her way, but the rights of mental patients are protected; she had that option. There was no reason for us to put a seventy-two-hour hold on her, she seemed well. Anyway, we called a cab for her and she informed us that she was returning home.'

'To her own house?'

'It was assumed she meant that. She chose a weekend to leave the hospital and it seems that all her family was out of town—that may have been deliberate on her part. With suicide in mind, she wouldn't have wanted interference. Of course we didn't know they were out of town, we merely knew we couldn't reach any of them by phone.'

'Do your records indicate that you were afraid of suicide?'

'No, to the contrary. Her therapist made a note after her death to the effect that such an act could not possibly have been anticipated. Although,' she added, 'just leaving Fernwood could have been unsettling. And then finding none of her family around—well, it seems to *me* she might very well have felt a moment of desperation and fear. But that's my opinion, not the psychiatrist's.'

'Makes sense to me. You're a therapist yourself?'

'No.' She flushed slightly. 'It's just that being around a place like this, you pick up things. I'm strictly on the administrative end of things.'

'So she seemed well and ready for a return to normal society?'

'That's what the records say. She had plans—' she glanced at the printout—'I won't go into them, but she seemed oriented towards a productive future.'

'And she went off and killed herself.'

She looked at him sadly. 'Yes. Drowned herself.'

'Well—' Pedersen and Tate made ready to leave—'we do thank you. There's nothing else in those notes that would be of use to us?'

'Probably a lot. But I can't give that information to you. You'd have to—'

'Subpœna it, I know.'

She walked to the front door with them. She moved sensuously; it was wonderful to Pedersen that a woman who seemed the embodiment of sex could be in her manner so down-to-earth. He turned to shake her hand and take in one more glimpse of her.

'Something!' he said to Tate as they walked to the car.

Tate shook his head. 'Yes, she's something, all right.'

'And all the friends of the family assumed Jane died after a bout with cancer,' Pedersen said as they pulled out of the driveway. 'Funny. People must have come to visit her.'

'I asked about that at Bay Cove Hospital. There, she didn't have visitors, aside from family. She was just there for a couple of weeks, I suppose they figured the depression would pass.'

'But not here. She was in the hospital for the better part of a year. We'll have to check it out with someone. Stanley Potter.'

Back at headquarters, Pedersen reached for the phone.

'Oh,' said Stanley Potter with a sigh, 'you've dug up all that business. We handled it the way we did because we thought it would be Jane's wish. She made us swear before she signed herself into Bay Cove that we wouldn't tell anyone.'

'But why? Is there such a stigma attached to being depressed? Unless—it was the suicide attempt?'

'Someone's told you about that.' There was a long silence. 'We're—we've all been a bit—' Stanley Potter made a sound deep in his throat—'sensitive on the subject.' After a moment he added, his voice constricted, 'Our mother was a suicide.'

'I see. I'm sorry. But people came to see her later—at Fernwood?'

'She relented and a couple of close friends visited. Not many. After a while even they dropped off. She asked us to make clear to her friends that she needed time to herself. She'd split up with her husband a while before and . . . Anyway, when she died, we let it be known that she'd had a brain tumour. That that accounted for her depression, her odd behaviour. No one knew about the suicide. We even told the kids in the family—Ann's children—that it was cancer. No point in having suicide hanging over them.'

As your mother's suicide hung over all of you, Pedersen thought. 'Ann's children never knew the cause of your mother's death, either?'

'No,' Stanley said roughly. 'It's not a subject we talk about. I really don't understand the relevance of all this to your investigation.'

'I need the facts,' Pedersen said flatly. 'Tell me about the finding of your sister Jane's body.'

'She—' Pedersen could hear him swallow hard—'was washed up north of town. We don't know it was suicide, it could just as well have been an accident. When she was well, she loved to walk by the water and she was always sitting out on the rocks. I don't have to tell you that people are washed off.'

'How long had she been dead?'

'About two weeks. The coroner said she probably died the day she got out of the hospital. Of course none of us knew she was out. The hospital tried to reach us to tell us she'd gone, but as luck had it, none of us was available. We didn't learn for a couple of days. By then she'd simply disappeared.'

'You called the police?'

'We thought about it, but in the end we hired a private detective. We were afraid of the publicity if we called the police. We assumed she was alive somewhere. And she'd been so adamant about no one knowing.'

'How did you come to find the body?'

'The detective. He checked the morgue every day and one afternoon he phoned Roy and me and asked us to come down there.'

'You were able to identify the body?'

'It was Jane all right, but she looked . . . It wasn't easy. We didn't let the girls see her—Ann and Kay.'

Pedersen paused and then asked the question. 'Was there any sign of foul play?'

'You think she was *killed*?'

Pedersen repeated his question.

'Jesus, you—No, the coroner said not. She looked—Do we *have* to go into all this?'

'I'm afraid we do. She looked?'

'Well, battered. But the coroner said that was just from being in the water so long and being knocked around among the rocks. God! You can imagine seeing someone close to you looking like that. When she was well, she had always been so fastidious. She would have hated it.'

'So you held the service as though she had died of cancer. With a closed casket.'

'Yes. Some of her friends were angry that they had never been able to visit or say goodbye, but they felt they'd honoured her wish. They all came to the memorial service, though. And she had masses of roses. She loved roses.'

'Your sister Ann didn't let Suzanne attend the service?'

'She thought she was too young. And Sue had been very fond of her aunt. Afterwards Ann read somewhere that it had been a mistake, that it's better to let kids experience the whole thing.'

Pedersen allowed a moment to pass before he asked, 'Your mother's suicide. When did that occur?'

Stanley Potter's voice was harsh. 'Right after my sister Kay was born.' He laughed, a bitter sound, 'Post-partum depression, no doubt.'

'You were how old?'

'Ten, just ten. A very young ten. Jane was eight and Roy was—six, I guess. Ann must have been about three.'

'It must have been hard on all of you.'

Stanley said nothing.

'I'm sorry we had to stir things up, Mr Potter, but it was necessary that we have this information.'

'I'm damned if I can see why. What has a nine-year-old suicide got to do with my sister's murder? Or my mother's death? It seems to me you're going about this investigation in a most peculiar way.' His voice had become cold.

'When is your sister Ann's service to be?' Pedersen hoped the change of subject would distract the man.

'Sunday at eleven. Episcopal church.' He sounded as icy as before.

Oh God, Pedersen thought as he hung up, we're going to get another complaint about my time-wasting, hassling ways. He turned to Tate triumphantly. 'I'll lay a bet that the letter Eugénie wrote was addressed to some member of Ann's family.'

'You think she was threatening to unearth all that old stuff, the mental hospital and the suicide and the family lying to everyone? How could she have known? And why would they have cared?'

'How she knew is still a question, but I don't think she was up to anything as innocuous as that.'

'Then what?'

'I think she wrote to say she had proof of murder. And she promised if they didn't come across, she'd take it to the police.'

CHAPTER 20

'Proof of murder! That's crazy. How could she have proof of a murder committed over nine years ago, even assuming there was such a murder? Carl, I think this time you've gone off the deep end.'

'But it follows. What if Jane Potter wasn't a suicide? What if she was murdered?'

'What happened to accident? She could have gone down to visit her old haunts, been sitting on a rock and been washed off.'

'We can check the weather for that day, see whether the waves were especially high. Although there seems a little uncertainty as to the exact day she died. And we need to see that coroner's report. But I—'

'Carl, you get these notions and you . . . cling to them. Now what's wrong with the idea that Eugénie was blackmailing the family over their shenanigans regarding the cancer and the mental illness? Though I can't even begin to imagine where she'd get such information.'

'That wouldn't be enough to get her killed. No one would be concerned. And who could she have told? The newspapers? Would the *Banner* have believed a vagrant who came to them with a story like that? Even if they did listen, who'd care about that stale old news?'

'The Potters and Koppleman and Brennan are prominent enough for it to have made a bit of nasty gossip.'

'The *Banner* wouldn't have listened. Anyway, they'd be risking a libel suit.'

Tate shook his head. 'It doesn't make sense. How, then, are you going to account for Ann Koppleman's murder? The murderer went after both the blackmailer *and* the blackmailee?'

'That's true, it doesn't answer the question of why Ann Koppleman was killed. Nothing seems to answer that.'

'Look at what you're saying. You're suggesting that Eugénie, a bag lady with no resources, no home, not even a sheet of paper and a stamp, would be able to garner information like that. Where? How?'

Pedersen grinned. 'You make me feel like an unreasonable teenager.'

Tate laughed. 'When you get these wild ideas, you sound like one, honest to God, Carl. At times like these, I feel years older than you.'

'But they sometimes turn out to be right, my wild hunches, don't they?'

'This won't be one of those times. I'll bet on it.'

'Maybe,' Pedersen said, returning to the subject, 'she was in the hospital with Jane Potter and got to know her.'

'No one remembered a Eugénie at Bay Cove Hospital.'

'It was ten years ago, they wouldn't remember. Maybe

she was there in some other capacity, as a nurse, for example. We don't know what she did before she turned up on the streets.'

Tate sighed. 'I can see we're going to pursue this.'

Pedersen laughed. 'Come on now, Ron, don't tell me you haven't the faintest suspicion that I could be right about Eugénie.'

'I agree that blackmail seems to be in the picture. The letter she wrote at the library. The phone call she could have made. The "surprise" she was planning. But I can't see it as the uncovering of murder. Or of a murderer.'

'But if it *were* of a murderer, what an excellent motive for him to murder again. Or her to murder again. What would he or she have to lose?'

'And Ann Koppleman?'

'You know, today you depress me, Ron.'

Ron Tate laughed. 'I know. I'm so rational.'

Pedersen grunted. 'Well, let's see if we can tie in Ann Koppleman's death.'

Tate groaned.

'She could—no. What if she were the one being blackmailed?'

'Yes? What if she were?'

'No, it doesn't work. Damn it, there must be some reason for her murder. Maybe it doesn't have anything to do with Eugénie, but there must be a reason.'

'She turned down Ollie?'

'But what would Oliver Winter be doing killing Eugénie?'

'Maybe one of her brothers or her sister killed Ann.'

'Again, no connection with Eugénie.'

'Unless—no, Eugénie wrote just the one letter, didn't she? Maybe she made some phone calls, too.' Tate took off his glasses and rubbed his eyes.

'What you're saying is she got in touch with all four of them? Where does that get us?'

'I don't know where it gets us. And they all deny having ever heard *of* Eugénie, much less having heard *from* her. I think we're on the wrong track, Carl, really I do. It just doesn't fit together, any of it.'

'I know.' Pedersen swivelled around and faced the window. 'You may be right. But I think the business of Jane Potter is in some way related to the deaths. It's the only link we have—a member of the family was a patient in the hospital and Eugénie hung around the hospital.'

'There's a little gap of some ten years there. And it's one of only two hospitals in town.'

'I know. You know, Ron, you should check Bay Cove Hospital to see whether there was a nurse named Eugénie there ten years ago.'

'I'll check, but I can tell you right now that unless she was a regular employee they won't have the information. Private nurses come and go, and I'm sure those records are incomplete.'

'Regular hospital staff, that's what I meant. Of course I'd feel on solider ground if we'd found some communication from Eugénie in Ann Koppleman's house. There wasn't a thing.'

'If someone were going to the trouble of killing her because of her connection with Eugénie, he'd take the trouble to destroy it, wouldn't he?'

'*That* could be the connection.' Pedersen swivelled his chair back to face Tate. 'Ann Koppleman receives a letter and decides to pay off Eugénie. Some member of her family gets wind of that and kills her and Eugénie, thereby removing all risk of exposure. No, it doesn't make sense.'

'It sounds more plausible than some of the other things you've been saying. Although I'd think just killing off Eugénie would have been adequate.'

'Overkill?' Pedersen laughed. 'No pun intended.'

'Who do we know who is connected with this case?' Tate asked. 'Stanley, Roy, Kay—the brothers and sister. Suzanne—the daughter. Jason, Ellery, Meredith—the sons.'

'The sons weren't here. Cross them off the list. Oliver

Winter, the boyfriend. Jedediah Martin, the other boyfriend. No, he's alibied. And Lewis Mawson, the doctor who hated Eugénie's guts and who knew Ann.'

'He knew her?' Tate asked.

'He'd met her at meetings and gatherings of benefactors.'

'That's interesting. He's the only person who's admitted an acquaintance with both of them.'

'Jedediah Martin was at the hospital, he was aware of Eugénie, and he knew Ann Koppleman. But he's out. His alibi is too tight.'

'Besides, what motive could either of them have for killing Eugénie? Or for that matter Ann? Rejection by her?'

'Mawson wasn't interested in Ann in that way, so far as I can tell. And that's not enough to warrant a stabbing. Ann seemed to have handled her affairs tactfully, she'd have let the man down gently, gradually.'

'But there comes a breaking-point. Maybe Ollie—'

Pedersen scooped up his worry beads from the desk where they lay and slammed them back down. 'Where does Eugénie fit in? In my scenario Ann doesn't fit in. In yours Eugénie doesn't. Let's let it lie. We've talked it into the ground.'

Tate sighed with relief. 'Wouldn't it be convenient if it were Lewis Mawson, an all round unpleasant person?'

Pedersen laughed. 'I'll go with that.' He dropped the worry beads in his pocket. 'I'll go with that.'

Tate's phone call came an hour later.

'There may have been a Eugénie. Someone remembered, an older charge nurse. She was a vocational nurse, that's what they call the bedside care nurses, and this woman is quite sure that was her name. She says she hasn't seen her in ages but she remembers that it was an unusual name, nobody could pronounce it. She couldn't recall anything about how she looked, but she did remember that she had worked with psychiatric patients. That could have been when Jane was a patient.'

'And Eugénie could have learned something and kept it to herself all those years. Far-fetched but possible.'

'Yes. Maybe a couple of years ago she heard the family had come into money and decided to cash in on it.'

'It seems crazy she'd wait all that time. What could she have learned? Do you suppose it was just coincidence, someone with the same name who nursed there?'

'We have to assume it isn't, don't we? It fits so neatly. It tells us, if it's the same Eugénie, how she got her information.'

'But what information? If it was something to do with Jane's death . . .' Pedersen sighed. 'And this head nurse was sure?'

'Pretty sure. Apparently she's allergic to French names.'

Pedersen grunted.

'The computer's down for repairs at the moment—'

'Of course.'

Tate grinned. 'But she said I could check the list of nurses as soon as it's fixed. We may actually come up with a *last* name.'

Pedersen grunted again.

CHAPTER 21

Rod MacMillan pushed his tray along the counter, wishing the woman at the end would make up her mind about dessert. He glanced at his wristwatch. He had scheduled a meeting for 1.30. That gave him three-quarters of an hour.

'Watch this now. She's not going to take either of them,' said a voice behind him.

He turned. 'Jerry. Isn't she something? God, now that guy's doing it. Ah, thank God, he's settled for the pie. Let's move while we can.'

'There should be separate cafeterias for patients' families,'

Jerry said as they walked away from the cashier. 'Or rather for us. Where do you want to sit?'

They found an empty table near a window.

Jerry picked up his soup spoon. 'What's happening in social work?'

Rod dumped dressing over his salad. 'The usual. Being low man on the totem pole is not a happy fate, and let me tell you, in a hospital social work is low man.'

'Physicians who don't take advantage of social workers should have their heads examined.'

'You realize you're alone in that opinion? Well, that's not true. There's such a split, though—some physicians really make use of my people but some won't let us get within feet of their patients. You've heard all this before. What's going on upstairs?'

'We have a kid who isn't going to make it. I have to tell his parents this afternoon.' He looked down at his tray. 'See how heartless we become? Eating a huge meal before giving those poor people the worst news of their lives.'

'That's rough, Jerry. If the parents'll accept help, send them down to us. I'll set them up with someone good.'

'I want to do that. I think they'll need it.' He finished his soup and began on his turkey sandwich. 'That lentil soup's the best thing the cafeteria makes.' He took another bite. 'Anything new on Eugénie?'

'I haven't heard anything. You?'

'Not much. Detectives around, I hear, checking hospital records and interviewing people. Lew was visited.'

'Mawson? No kidding. Wonder what they asked him.'

'I wonder if they know he sees Ann Koppleman's sister.'

'What? He knows that family? How do you know?'

'I know her by sight. She's Kay Brennan, a high-stepping gal who I hear has some sort of Open Marriage. She shows up here and there, usually with Lew. They're Good Friends.'

'Does he know you've seen him with her?'

'Would he care? But I doubt that he knows. As a general rule he doesn't see me, especially when I'm with my wife.

He remembers who I am at meetings. Between times he looks through me.'

Rod put down his fork and leaned forward. 'Maybe you should tell one of those detectives.'

'What? Are you off your rocker? Why would I do that?'

'Maybe he has some connection with—' he looked around and lowered his voice—'the murders.'

'Rod, what are you talking about? Just because he's making it with the sister?'

'Jerry, the rumour is that they were killed by someone with medical training. It was a surgeon's cut.'

Rod stared at him. 'You think Mawson—?'

'He's pretty flaky. And he would have had to rotate through surgery during his training.' He wondered if he should tell Jerry the other thing he knew about Mawson.

'Listen, he's a bastard, I grant you that, and a snob and supercilious and generally uncooperative, but a murderer—that's insane.'

'He's one psychiatrist that went into his field out of his own neurotic needs, let me tell you. He has all the earmarks.'

'Maybe he did, but that doesn't make him a murderer, not by a long shot.' He grinned. 'You sound a little flaky yourself on this subject.'

'I suppose I do.'

'You just hate Mawson.'

Rod mopped salad dressing from his plate with French bread. 'I don't hate him. Yes, you know I do. I don't know why I should.'

Jerry smiled. 'Maybe he reminds you of your father.'

Rod laughed. 'I liked my old man, it can't be that. Tell me, how is Mawson with a woman? I mean, how does he treat her? Is he arrogant with women, too?'

'I ran into him at this party—one of the men in cardiology had an Open House. Really open, too, all departments represented.'

'And in every corner was a group discussing its specialty.'

Jerry laughed. 'You've got it. Only not Mawson. Kay

Brennan was strictly in charge, she didn't leave his side. He was . . . very attentive.'

'Not arrogant?'

'If so, it wasn't visible. He gave the impression of being the doting lover. I *assume* lover. I can't see Lew spending time with a woman who doesn't put out.'

Rod finished his baked apple. 'I'm still hungry, I should have had some of that lentil soup. Well, that must have been something to witness.'

'It was—interesting. Made me wonder if Lew's façade conceals a totally different sort of person.'

'A pussycat? Whatever it is, it could only be an improvement. I'm going to have to take off. I've called a meeting for one-thirty. I still think you should pass on the information—' He caught Jerry's expression. 'OK, forget it. He's a pussycat, I'll remember that next time he's telling off one of my social workers.'

But, he told himself as he stacked his tray and dumped his silver into the bin, if those detectives interview me, *I'll* tell them about Kay Brennan. And maybe about the other, the time he had found him, with Eugénie asleep, touching her that way. Eugénie through some miracle hadn't wakened, probably so fagged out she didn't feel a thing, and Mawson had talked fast. The guy had seemed to him genuinely ashamed of what he called his 'impulse', and Rod had finally let him off the hook, promised him he wouldn't tell anyone. But he had never looked Mawson straight in the eye. People didn't do those things out of the blue, there was a history, but he'd never heard anything else out of line. Probably that one experience had scared him shitless.

But now, now that he realized the guy knew the Kopple-man family as well, the whole thing took on a different colouration. He'd have to think about it.

CHAPTER 22

Suzanne Ford locked her car door and, conscious of how tired she was, slowly began to climb the hill from the parking lot to the building in which her class met. She didn't feel right about coming back so soon, but she'd missed the last meeting of this class and she couldn't afford two in a row. She supposed one afternoon class wasn't like coming back in earnest, all day every day. She'd do that next week after the service was over.

At the top of the hill she ran into a classmate, Mary Beth. 'Oh, Sue, what an *awful* thing,' Mary Beth began. 'I read—oh dear, I didn't mean to make you cry.' Awkwardly she fished in her pocket and dragged out a clean, crumpled tissue with which she presented Suzanne.

Suzanne scrubbed at her eyes, which immediately filled again. 'It's all right. I probably shouldn't have tried to come to class so soon. I thought it might get my mind off things.'

'Here, let me walk with you.' They mounted the steps to the second floor. 'I just—I guess you'd rather not talk about it.' But her curiosity got the best of her. 'Your place must be *swarming* with police.'

'No. A detective came by a couple of times. I know they're working on it, trying to find out—'

'Who did it? That was awfully odd, that woman at the hospital who was killed too, wasn't it? Did your mother know her? I mean, your mother was involved with some charities, wasn't she?'

'Not charities, exactly. And I don't think she'd ever met the woman, I think it was just some crazy—You know, Mary Beth, I really can't talk about it. What did I miss Tuesday?'

'That's right, you weren't in class. He talked about—

cripes, I'll have to look at my notes. You were at your mother's house?'

'No, they didn't locate me till dinner-time. I was in the library, doing some research.'

'No kidding! You mean you deliberately cut class? That must have been a first for you. You never cut classes, do you?'

'I figured it was the one time I could get at the books that are on reserve for this class, the ones we can't take out. It worked.'

'Clever, clever. I'll have to try that.'

They opened the door and seated themselves in the back of the still empty classroom. 'Now, if you'd let me see those notes, Mary Beth.'

'I guess you don't want to talk about it,' said Mary Beth, riffling through the pages of her notebook.

'That's the idea,' said Suzanne. 'That's the idea.' She began to copy the notes.

Stanley Potter, when he thought of it, marvelled that he had come such a long way. True, he was no longer young, although he was, he reminded himself, still a virile and handsome man, but none the less his progress was remarkable. Who would have guessed he'd become a major partner in a firm as substantial as this one? When he had really been young, he had been confused, directionless. All those false starts—what was the old rhyme: doctor, lawyer, merchant, chief? That had been him. Roy, on the other hand, had always had a knack with art and had settled into his field without any fuss. But he—Stanley remembered his father's anger over his indecisiveness. He sighed. He and his father had never come to terms on the subject of profession. They had never come to terms, period.

Well, he had, as the saying went, found himself when he came into business. Business, in particular the software industry, involved him as nothing else had. His partners had for a time dominated the scene, that was true, but that had ended with his investment of the inheritance. The old man had done one good thing for him, at least. And the company had rebounded; the infusion of new money had turned them around. He had seen the glances they threw his way when figures were discussed these days, and he had noticed the new respect in the way in which they addressed him. Nothing in his life had given him such satisfaction. If it weren't for Ann's death, he could be completely happy. Ann's death was constantly with him.

When he thought about himself he realized he had been unsure, always, he supposed. He sat at his desk in the new office and thought about it. He didn't know why it had been that way. As the eldest child and a boy, he must have been welcomed, but—he winced at the memory—his first recollection was of reaching out to grasp his little sister's arm and having his mother slap him hard. Immediately after, she had pulled him to her. Her face was wet. But it left a wound. That, and even more, the difference in his father's attitude towards his little sister. He still felt a slight chill when he thought of his father, even three years after his death.

His father had been a cold man, cold to him at any rate. And to Roy too, now he thought of it. Just not there for them. Absent. His father liked girls. Everything had been plummy for the girls in the family, all they had to do was look pretty and say 'yes' to their father and they could have anything. It probably accounted for their confidence, their making marriages so easily, while he and—But that was their mother's suicide, too. Objectively, he supposed he was suffering from what the shrinks would call a classic fear of abandonment, but subjectively . . . He could never think of his mother with real emotion. There was a sort of blank where filial feeling should be. You left me, I feel nothing for you, was what it added up to. It was as though something essential in him had been choked off. He guessed the same had happened to Roy.

But this new success—sometimes he felt he had spent his

life realizing his father's prediction that he would fail. Fail at studies, fail at work. He wished the old man were here now to see that he had made it, finally, that he was looked to for decisions, admired, sought out by his colleagues. It was a slightly hollow victory, as though it had come a lifetime too late, but he *had* it at last, that was the important thing.

And Martha. Now and then he thought of calling Martha, he'd heard she was widowed and alone, but something made him hesitate.

The thought of Martha damped down his spirits. He applied himself to the work at hand in an effort to put her out of his mind. But she kept popping into his consciousness, Martha with her dark eyes and gipsyish clothing. She had been a strange choice of lover for him, so different in every way, but she lent excitement to everything they did. She had an adventurousness he had never encountered, probably because women like Martha took one look at him and, buttoned down as he was, thought: Why bother? But if he had to say it himself, he had depths. There were aspects to his personality that he hadn't even known existed until he met Martha. Maybe that was what had scared him away.

On impulse, he pulled the phone towards him. Why *not* call? He could give her his condolences, rather late but still . . . He had to check her number; it had been years, literally, since they had spoken.

She answered on the fifth ring, just as he was about to give up. She must have run in from out of doors, she was a gardener. 'Yes? Let me get my breath.' After a moment she said, 'OK, I'm all right now.'

'It's Stan, Martha.'

There was a long pause, then she said, her voice low, 'Stanley. It's been a long time.'

'Yes. You—I hear you . . .'

'Yes, I lost Holman over a year ago. I'm all right,' she added as though he had asked.

Stanley felt relief. He wasn't sure how he would have

coped with an expression of grief over another man. 'Good, Martha. Good. I wondered if we might see each other, have dinner or something. Would that work for you?' He realized he had expressed himself as though he were talking with a business associate. 'I mean, would you like to do that?'

She laughed. 'Would I! Stanley, I've been thinking about you, hoping you would call. Two minds with but a simple thought.'

He was astonished at how relaxed he had suddenly become. 'Tonight, Martha?'

'Tonight's fine, Stanley. I read about your . . . trouble. About Ann. That's really dreadful. You must be so upset.'

'We are. I . . . found her.' Hastily he went on, 'The police are working on it. I'm sure they'll come up with something.' After a moment he added, his tone grim, 'That doesn't make the loss any the less.'

'No, I'm sure it doesn't. And what's this odd business of the vagrant who was killed the same day? Do the police connect the two?'

'It seems the knives—' he found it hard to talk about, even to think of—'were exactly the same, or something. The—what do they call it?—*modus operandi* matched.'

'Strange, almost as though the killer were calling attention to the connection.'

Was that what it was that accounted for the labels left on the knives? Before he had time to respond, she asked, 'Was she one of Ann's stray kittens?'

For a moment Stanley was taken aback, as though she had meant that literally. But of course she couldn't have known Ann was a collector of stray kittens as a child. 'You mean someone she worked with? No, she wasn't. Ann worked at Marigold House, that's abused women.'

'Well, it's strange all the same. What time, Stanley?'

'Tonight? Seven?'

'Fine.' Her voice soft, she added, 'It will be lovely to see you again.'

As he hung up he felt congested, positively congested

with happiness. He couldn't catch his breath properly. Everything was turning out right for him. The business doing well, his position in the firm solid, Martha eager to see him. Well, not everything. A chill touched him. There was Ann's death, that awful moment when he had entered her bedroom, it was always on the periphery of his mind.

He missed her. If he hadn't missed her so much, he wondered if he ever would have called Martha again. Maybe one good thing had come out of her murder, he thought sadly.

CHAPTER 23

'Did you catch the murderer?' Freda asked. She was smiling.

'What murderer? Oh, *that* murderer. Of course I did, that's why I'm home early.' He rummaged in his Nut Drawer for a packet of peanuts. 'How about a drink?'

She looked at him doubtfully. 'You didn't really catch him, did you?'

'Not a chance. This is going to take time. The usual?'

She nodded. 'You did find out some new things, though?'

'We found out that Jane Potter didn't die of cancer, she was a suicide.'

'Jane Potter? Did you tell me about her?'

'She, I think, is the link I've been looking for.' He handed her the drink and picked up his vermouth. 'Let's go sit for a few minutes, I'm beat.'

He swung his feet up to the hassock of his favourite chair. 'That's more like it. Want some peanuts?'

'Carl, when do I ever want peanuts? Tell me who Jane Potter is.'

'She was Ann Koppleman's sister and she died some nine or ten years ago from drowning. She had been a patient at Bay Cove and then she was transferred to a small private hospital.'

She curled her feet under her and settled into a corner of the sofa. 'That makes her a link? Because Eugénie chose that hospital to sleep in?'

'No, it's not that.' He explained what they had turned up during the day's efforts.

'Sounds pretty far out to me.'

'Freda, please. Ron spent the afternoon explaining to me that I'm totally unreasonable. I hoped for better things from you.'

She laughed. 'Know what I did today?'

'Auditioned for a new play?'

'No, there aren't any auditions this month.'

'Took on a new client?'

'You're getting warm.'

He took a sip of his drink and leaned back in his chair. 'I give up.'

'I attended a workshop. Do you know, Carl—' she leaned forward, her face intent—'I never realized I was competitive. Did you?'

Her husband put his head back and laughed. 'You, competitive?'

'Don't laugh, I'm serious. We talked about things we had done that gave us particular satisfaction and experiences that had troubled us. You know what gave me satisfaction? Beating Marilee Wilson in the ninth grade essay contest. It was the first thing that popped into my head. And what troubled me was not getting the lead in the last play. Doesn't that mean I'm competitive?'

'Or human.'

'Is it human to want to beat other people out at things?'

'We have it drilled into us, don't we? Be best. Beat them. Win, win, win.'

'Then I'm not competitive?'

'Oh, I wouldn't say that.' He looked across the room at her with a slight smile on his face. 'You like all this soul-searching you do at the Centre, don't you?'

She nodded. 'You know, I do. I think I like talking

about myself.' She darted a glance at him. 'That makes me narcissistic as well as competitive, doesn't it?'

'You know anybody who doesn't like talking about himself?'

'Some of the counsellors say they don't. They feel these sessions are intrusive. One woman left the Centre because she didn't like the workshops.'

'Just how are they supposed to help you?'

'You untangle yourself so you can be more useful to the clients. Well, to anybody, I suppose.'

'Like me?'

'I'm quite useful enough to you. Aren't I?' she added, with a little anxiety in her voice.

'What do you do for me?'

'I get dinner for you. That is, when you're rested enough to come out and help chop vegetables for the salad.'

He sighed. 'I knew there was a catch.' He studied the contents of his glass. 'I'm going to have to do more with Jane Potter.'

'Like what?'

'Go back and talk to the social worker and the head of Psychiatry at Bay Cove, see if they know anything at all about her death.'

'Why should they if she was at another place when she died?'

'I imagine when hospitals make referrals they keep in touch. Bay Cove may be more forthcoming than Fernwood.' He finished off his drink and set the glass aside. 'The last thing we did today was check the coroner's report on her. She was in perfect health, simply inhaled a quantity of water. Drowned. No signs of strangulation or beating. He noted that she'd been buffeted about during the two weeks she'd been in the water, but none of the injuries were consistent with the assumption of foul play.'

'And despite all that, you think she was killed? Why?'

'Mostly because it would be such an excellent motive for murdering Eugénie.'

'If she was blackmailing her murderer.'

'Yes. Of course that doesn't account for Ann Kopple-man's death. Nothing seems to account for both deaths. If we figure out a motive for one, it doesn't work with the other. And vice versa,'

'It must be hard to find out about someone who's been dead as long as Jane Potter.'

'It is. And her having spent the better part of a year in hospitals affects things, too. If she'd been at home, there might have been journals, writings that had been kept. People would have noticed things. Hospitals have records, but they're clinical, not personal. And they won't let me have access to them, not without a subpœna. Well—' he broke open a peanut and checked for the dwarf as he had done with his father when he was a boy—'let's go chop vegetables so you can be useful to me.'

CHAPTER 24

Rod MacMillan was in conference in his office when Pedersen and Tate arrived. Waiting under the eye of Mac-Millan's secretary, they were silent. They had deliberately chosen to come in without appointment, and when the door from the office opened after ten minutes and MacMillan and his visitor emerged, the social worker looked surprised, almost taken aback.

He saw his visitor to the door of the waiting-room and returned. 'More questions?' He looked at Tate with curi-osity.

'A few. This is Detective Tate. He's working on the case with me.'

MacMillan led them into his office. Empty coffee-cups sat on his desk. 'Just had a cup, but I could stand another. Would you care for coffee?'

Pedersen and Tate shook their heads. 'We just had some, too,' Tate said.

MacMillan pulled up a second chair, pushed the mugs aside and sat down at his desk. 'What can I tell you?'

'Mr MacMillan, how long have you been with the hospital?'

'Let's see, it's—God, it's twelve years now. I had one other job, worked for five years with a Los Angeles hospital. My wife and I wanted out of L.A. and when the assistant directorship opened up here, I applied, thinking I'd never get it. But they liked something about my résumé, my big city experience, I guess. I came on as assistant and when the director left eight years ago, I took over.'

'So you were here ten years ago, when Jane Potter was a patient?'

MacMillan threw him an odd look. 'Jane Potter? You're interested in her? I thought—'

'Yes, we're investigating two totally different lives, but we're looking for links between the two. Jane Potter was Ann Koppleman's sister.'

MacMillan looked astonished. 'She was? I never connected the two.'

'I see you remember Jane Potter, though. How is that?'

'She was a suicide, did you know that? When she signed herself out of Fernwood—that's the hospital she was transferred to from here—a psychiatric social worker I know who worked there and had seen her told me he thought she was in good shape, no longer depressed or suicidal. We'd worried about suicide right along when she was here, you see. There'd been an attempt before she came in.'

'The family didn't mention that. We learned it at Fernwood.'

'At any rate my friend was terribly upset over their misjudgement of her condition. He felt he was partially responsible. He'd had a good relationship with her, you see, and he felt if he'd made a correct assessment, he could have talked her out of leaving right then. He talked about it so much during our next few visits that—'

'It fixed it in your mind.'

'That and the suicide itself. The brother apparently made accusations, said Fernwood had behaved irresponsibly and so on. Of course, it was her perfect right to sign herself out. The family didn't try to sue, but they'd have lost if they had. The law protects mental patients these days.'

'Sometimes to their detriment, I'd say, judging by some of the people on the mall,' Tate commented drily.

'Yes, but you wouldn't want it the other way. Now what can I tell you about Jane Potter? We must have records here.'

'Good. I suppose you can't let me see them?'

'Not unless they're subpœnaed. But I can check for you, if there's something in particular, and if it isn't highly confidential.'

Pedersen's smile was disarming. 'Since I don't know quite what it is I'm looking for, maybe you'd get out the records and glance over them with an eye to spotting anything out of the ordinary.'

'Everything about a mental patient is out of the ordinary. May I ask—that is—'

'You want to know what it is that we have in mind regarding her?'

'Well—' MacMillan smiled—'it might help me to know what I'm looking for.'

'I'd prefer that you regard this as confidential, but we're considering the possibility that she was murdered.'

'She too? Isn't that a little excessive?'

Pedersen laughed. 'My partner here thinks so. But that's what interests us. Me, that is.'

MacMillan rang his secretary. 'Jean, will you dig out records on Jane Potter? That'll have been closed out about eight years ago.'

'Ten,' Pedersen corrected.

'That's ten, Jean.' He rang off.

'While we're waiting,' he said, 'I'm going to give you a piece of gossip, hearsay that may have absolutely no bearing on the case. But since you're looking for links . . .' He hesitated, as though he had thought better of the impulse.

After a minute he said, 'You know, I should have connected Ann Koppleman and Jane Potter. The name rang a faint bell, but I figured that was because her name was in the papers occasionally. Anyway, what I was going to tell you . . .'

'Yes?' Pedersen encouraged.

'Jerry'll murder me if he finds out I told you, but I feel you should know, although I'm having second thoughts—Oh, what the hell, I'm going to tell you. Lewis Mawson, the psychiatrist whom I understand you interviewed, is one of Kay Brennan's escorts. Now that I say it,' he added, 'it doesn't seem too relevant.'

'One of her escorts?' Tate said. 'I understood she was married.'

'I gather she has an Open Marriage. Remember them?'

'The O'Neills' book, yes,' said Tate. 'I thought that had gone out of style, what with herpes and AIDS on everyone's mind.'

MacMillan grinned. 'So she's old-fashioned. Anyway, for what it's worth, I've given you the information.' He hesitated. 'Something else—'

A knock at the door drew his attention. 'Ah, Jean, thank you. That was fast.'

Alone with Pedersen and Tate again, MacMillan opened the folder. 'In a general way, I can fill you in. She came to us after the suicide attempt—'

'How did she go about it?' Pedersen asked.

'The usual, sleeping pills. She was depressed, cried a lot and just sat. Brooded. Or slept. Dysfunctional for the most part, although functional enough so that she saw she needed help.'

'Her family may have influenced that,' Tate contributed.

'I'm sure they did. She had lots of family visits throughout her ten days here, but Ann was the most frequent visitor.'

Pedersen raised eyebrows. 'So they were close.'

'It seems so, although the caseworker says here that she always seemed more depressed after Ann's visits.'

'That's interesting. Anything else?'

'No, I've told you more than I should have as it is. I didn't realize the family hadn't let you in on the suicide attempt. I shouldn't have mentioned that.'

Tate turned to Pedersen. 'But it bears out the assumption that her death was by suicide.'

'Yes, it does.' Pedersen sighed. 'At any rate, thanks for your time and for what you've given us. Just before your secretary came in, you started to say something. You were going to tell us something else.'

'You're going to see Mawson again?'

Pedersen nodded. 'As a matter of fact, we are. There was something else about him?'

'No.' MacMillan looked down at the folder in his hands. 'I don't recall what I was going to say. But for God's sake—' he looked up again—'don't let on to Mawson that I told you about him and Kay. Maybe you shouldn't mention it at all, he may remember that Jerry was at some of the same parties.'

'We may have to mention it. We'll let it be assumed it came from outside the hospital.'

'I hope you convince him. I *am* having second thoughts now that it's too late. Jerry was right.'

'Dr Cohen thought you shouldn't pass the information on to us?'

'He didn't think it had anything to do with anything. And probably it doesn't.'

'No, probably not, but the links between the hospital and the Potter-Koppleman-Brennan crowd grow stronger, don't they?' Pedersen rose to leave. 'It may not be relevant, but it's interesting. And if you think of what you wanted to tell us, give me a ring.' He dropped his card on the desk.

MacMillan picked it up and said nothing.

As he and Tate left the office, Pedersen turned to his partner. 'The plot thickens,' he said. He smiled.

Tate groaned.

Lewis Mawson's secretary made clear that Dr Mawson had no time for further visits from the police. 'Didn't you see him just yesterday?' she asked, addressing Tate, her voice as pained as though they were tiresome patients making untoward and impossible demands.

'Yes. When will he be free?' Pedersen asked.

She pursed her lips. '*Really!* He'll be finished with his patient in—' she checked her watch—'five minutes, but he—'

'That's fine,' Pedersen interrupted. 'We'll wait.' He and Tate seated themselves.

After a period of time the secretary rang through to Mawson. Despite her lowered tone and turned head, they picked up the tenor of her communication: 'detectives again . . . know how busy you are . . . yes, I'll tell them.' She swung around and raised her voice slightly. 'You may go in, but Dr Mawson can give you just a *very* few minutes.'

'Isn't his patient in there?' Tate asked.

She regarded him without expression. 'The patients use the other door,' she said.

Mawson consulted his watch as they entered, controlled outrage evident on his face. 'You seem to be making a habit of this. It had better be brief, I have work to do,' he announced. He did not offer them seats.

Pedersen strolled over to the chair nearest the desk and sat down. Tate took another chair. 'Dr Mawson,' Pedersen said, once the physician had with an irritable gesture seated himself behind his desk, 'today we're here to talk with you about an old patient.'

'Jane Potter again.' His face expressed disgust. 'Someone was here, you—' he indicated Tate—'yesterday. I told you she'd been transferred out of here some years ago and I later heard she committed suicide. That's all there is.'

'Today, however, we'd like you to consult your records of her therapy sessions.'

'That's ridiculous, those records are confidential! I'm not about to share them with you.'

'We'll have to subpœna them in their entirety unless you share *some* information with us, Doctor,' Pedersen said. His voice was gentle but he knew Mawson heard the underlying resolution.

Mawson shrugged irritably. 'What is it you want to know? I don't understand your interest in a years-old suicide.'

'Jane Potter was Ann Koppleman's sister.'

'I'm aware of that—that is, your detective made me aware of it yesterday. I had forgotten.'

'Oh?' Pedersen's eyebrows went up. He let the silence extend a moment beyond comfort. 'We understood that you were a friend of the family.'

Mawson's reaction was so strong that Pedersen glanced at Tate to see if he had caught the fear that crossed the physician's face.

'You're mistaken,' Mawson said coldly.

'Then just a friend of Mrs Brennan's, is that it?'

Mawson stood up abruptly. 'I think you go beyond yourself. How do you justify inquiring into my personal affairs?'

Pedersen turned a mild face towards him. 'Inquiring into your personal affairs? I'd hardly say that. A casual remark by one of the family—'

'That's a lie! No one knows—' He stopped, his face congested by rage. 'What is it you want from me—that's within your province of inquiry? What do you want to know about Jane Potter?'

'We're interested in her last few sessions. You were the treating physician?'

'No, I wasn't, as a matter of fact.' Mawson re-seated himself. 'However, I can check her therapist's notes.' His voice was cold. 'What exactly am I to tell you about the last sessions?'

'Primarily whether she was troubled about something or

someone in particular. Maybe her sister, for example. In a word, whether her therapist regarded her as still suicidal.'

Mawson again looked at his watch. He reached for the button on the intercom. 'Miss Roberts, get out Jane Potter's record. She was discharged nine or ten years ago. That's P-O-T-T-E-R.'

They waited in silence.

The record before him, Mawson glanced down and then back at Pedersen. 'Who is your superior officer?'

Pedersen told him. As he watched Mawson note the name, he reflected with amusement that he was accumulating an extraordinary number of complaints on this case.

Mawson opened the folder, turning pages rapidly. Towards the last of the sheets enclosed within it, he slowed and read. After a time he closed the folder and looked up. 'She was not in good spirits. At the time she was transferred, she was seen as still being profoundly depressed. Any reference to specific troubled feelings, I would be unable to share with you.'

'Did her sister Ann figure in those troubled feelings?'

'Yes, but that is absolutely all I can say.'

'After her suicide, did her therapist add anything? Any addendum?'

'As a matter of fact he did. He added a note, pointing out that mood swings are common after a long hospitalization. He felt the family had been remiss in its attention to her on her return home.'

'Wasn't he aware that she did *not* return home?'

'Apparently not. We can't know everything. He did make a note expressing disapproval of Fernwood's releasing her on her own, without family there, but she was within her rights.'

'Interesting. May I have the name of the treating physician?'

'He's long since moved on.' There was triumph in Mawson's voice. 'He's working on the East Coast.' Where you can't get at him, his tone said.

'And you're sure there was no particular expression of concern or ambivalence towards anyone in those last sessions?'

'Oh, ambivalence, that's stock with patients in therapy. And I mentioned her sister. But absolutely nothing out of the ordinary. For a depressed patient, that is.'

'No hint, no clue as to her future behaviour.'

'The suicide? Nothing specific.'

'Well then, I guess that's all for now, Doctor.' Pedersen rose and Tate followed suit. 'I'm sorry I upset you with the reference to Mrs Brennan.'

'Upset me! You didn't *upset* me. It's none of your damned business whom I see and where and when. Keep your inquiries to police concerns. That's something I'd have thought you'd have learned by now.'

'It was an innocent remark, Dr Mawson. Made in passing. If I'd realized it was something you feel so strongly about, I certainly wouldn't have made it.' He stopped, one hand on the doorknob. 'Is there anything else you'd care to tell us? About yourself, I mean.'

Mawson froze. 'What do you mean? Did someone—' He checked himself.

'Anything?'

'I've no idea what you're talking about.' The physician eyed them coldly. 'Are you done? Well then, get out.'

'We're on our way. Thank you for your help.' His back to Mawson, Pedersen caught Tate's eye and winked. Then they were through the door, into the waiting-room and past the formidable Miss Roberts.

'There's something there,' Pedersen said, now sober, as they walked down the hall.

'There's always something. With everyone,' Tate said.

'Yes. That's true.' But Pedersen was quiet as they left the hospital.

'You did get his back up,' Tate remarked as they reached the car.

'Yes, Harbison's going to get another complaint. I'm

going to get myself taken off this case if I don't watch it.'

'I doubt that.'

'You caught the expression on Mawson's face when I raised the issue of acquaintance with the family?'

'Yes. Why should he be *afraid*?'

'And of what? Or should that be of whom?'

'It's crazy. There seems to be a lot more than meets the eye in this case. And the connections—here we were complaining about seeing no connections, now we can't see anything but.'

'It would be nice if we understood them.'

'Yes, it would.'

'We still don't see how Eugénie fits in,' Pedersen said. 'Except for how she got her information for blackmail.'

'If that's what it was. You don't suppose, do you, that she had Mawson on her hit list? Maybe that's why he disliked her in that irrational way.'

'Except,' said Pedersen, 'irrational seems to describe most of his reactions, it wouldn't take blackmail. Wouldn't you like to be one of his patients?'

Tate gave a mock shudder.

'If I could think what to ask her,' said Pedersen, 'I'd go see Kay Brennan.'

Tate pulled into the police parking lot. 'You could say, "What do you do to the good doctor that frightens him so?"'

'Or, "What do you know that scares him so?"'

'I suppose a fishing expedition might turn something up.'

'We could try. I doubt it, though. I have an idea she'd say, "Why, of course Lewis Mawson is my good friend. Whatever can anyone make of that?" Or words to that effect.'

'So what now?'

Pedersen turned the key in the ignition. 'Oh, what the hell. Let's go try Kay Brennan.'

CHAPTER 25

Kay Brennan was at the moment engaged in animated conversation.

She held the phone away from her ear. 'Lew, for Christ's sake, stop shouting at me. I thought you didn't want to have any personal conversation from the hospital.'

'Fuck that! Anyway, Roberts has gone off to lunch and the switchboard isn't taking calls yet.' He went on: 'You're going to be visited by the police again, I'm sure of it, and I just want to make sure you know what to say.'

'What *not* to say, you mean.'

'They sprung this friend-of-the-family bit on me and I lost my cool completely. One of us has to behave—'

'Rationally? Nonchalantly? You can count on me, I'm an expert at nonchalance.'

'You'd better be.'

'That sounds vaguely like a threat. Are you threatening me, Lewis? Because I believe I have more room to make threats than you.'

'Of course I'm not threatening you.' He paused; she could tell he was controlling his anger.

'How do you manage with your patients' problems, Lew? You get so . . . wrought up.'

'I don't get wrought up with patients.' His voice was cold. 'We've discussed this.'

'Oh yes, the Professional Self versus the Personal Self. When you get upset like this I forget that.'

'Kay, are you deliberately trying to be irritating?'

She laughed. 'Maybe. I don't like having you phone to tell me what to say and what not to say. It seems disrespectful. As though you don't trust me to make adequate judgements on my own.'

'All right. Save the sarcasm. Do you think we should still meet tonight?'

'Of course. Does a visit from the police frighten you that much?'

'It doesn't frighten me, it makes me uneasy. I'll see you at seven, then. But be careful—'

'What I say. Yes. I got the message. See you later, Lew, darling.' With amusement she heard her deliberately lilting tones. Screw you, doctor, she thought. I'll say any damned thing I please to anyone I damned please. Once all this mess over Ann's death is done, you, Lewis, will have to go. The thought was followed by an engulfing wave of relief.

The police were predictable; shortly after Lewis's alert, they arrived. This time the younger one, the one who had accompanied Pedersen that first day at the house, was along. She liked his looks: tall, thin as a blade, intelligent-looking with his wire-rimmed glasses, dressed like a young college professor. She turned to him. He looked a sympathetic sort.

'Lewis tells me you'll be asking me some questions.' She had decided to disarm them.

He was startled by her directness, she could tell. He gave her a searching look. 'Yes, we want to do that.' Pedersen had stepped back, so he went on. 'We understand you and Dr Mawson are good friends.'

'We are.' She looked up into his face. 'We are. Good friends.'

'Dr Mawson seemed disturbed that we should mention your friendship.'

She continued to gaze up at him. 'Is that a question? Or am I supposed to say something revealing in answer to your non-question?'

Pedersen spoke. 'Can you tell us, is Dr Mawson acquainted with the rest of the family? Did he know your sister Ann, by any chance?'

'He's met them all at least once. Once in a while we wind

up at the same restaurant as one of my brothers or my sister—we *did*, that is. Lewis is hardly a friend of the family.'

They moved into the pastel and white living-room. 'This will sound odd,' Tate said, 'but has he any reason to be afraid—' he obviously didn't know how to go on—'about any aspect of his acquaintance with you or your family?'

'Afraid?' She was thrown slightly off balance. Her directness was one thing, but this policeman's was another. Did they know about Lew? If they did, she'd better align herself with them against his kinkiness. God knows, she *was* against it. She checked herself in time. That was ridiculous, they couldn't know. She repeated the word. 'Afraid? Afraid of what? What is there to be afraid of?'

'We don't know. Frankly, we were disconcerted. We couldn't tell whether or not he knew something about your sister's death—or maybe your other sister's death.'

'My *other* sister?' For a moment she couldn't think what he was talking about. 'Oh. You mean Jane. But she died ten years ago.'

'Cancer?' asked Pedersen.

Something in his face caught her up short. 'Not exactly. Although we let it be understood it was cancer. Actually, she killed herself.'

'Killed herself?'

'Yes.' Suddenly she was angry at this inquisition. This was the sort of stuff Stanley had warned them against, this sort of questioning. 'What has she got to do with anything?' she said. 'What are you doing about *Ann's* death, that's the question.'

Pedersen answered. 'Actually, we're finding the going rather difficult. We haven't a motive for your sister's death and while we can imagine a motive for the death of the other woman, Eugénie, we can't understand why someone would murder both her and your sister.'

She took a cigarette from the box on the coffee table. She hadn't smoked in months, but suddenly she needed one as she had never needed one. All this was getting to her.

'You've absolutely stricken out the idea that these were unrelated killings?'

'No,' Tate said. 'But we think they're related.'

Inhaling deeply, she found she was dizzy with pleasure and with the unfamiliar smoke in her lungs. The younger detective noticed. 'Are you all right, Mrs Brennan?'

'Yes. Just my first cigarette in months.' She realized as soon as she said it that it was a confession that she was disturbed. With tremendous effort, she stubbed out the cigarette. 'Guess I don't want it after all.' She felt slightly nauseated.

'Mrs Brennan,' Pedersen said, 'was there ever a suggestion of foul play in your sister Jane's death?'

'You mean someone pushed her off the rocks?' For a fleeting moment she felt the clutch of fear; she wondered if the detective had seen it in her face. 'No, no. My sister was a mental patient. Deeply depressed. It was suicide.'

Pedersen persisted. 'The records indicate that she was not depressed when she signed herself out of the hospital. In fact she seemed in high spirits when she got into a cab to come home.'

'Home?' To her ears the question sounded stupid.

'Whatever she meant by home. Didn't she have a house?'

'No. I mean yes, but she had rented it—or we had when she seemed in for a long stay at Fernwood.' At Tate's glance, she explained, 'It was rented on a monthly basis only. But she wouldn't have gone there. She wouldn't have gone there,' she repeated.

'You had anticipated a long hospitalization?'

'We weren't sure, but it was an expensive house. We rented it to cover costs.'

'Mortgage, you mean?'

'And gardener. Maintenance.'

'Did insurance cover her hospitalization?'

'Partly. She had money, it wasn't that. But she wasn't living in the house—'

Pedersen broke in. 'Let's put aside the matter of the

house. You say your sister had money. Did she leave a will?'

'Actually, she did. We were rather surprised, she left everything to us. Of course there wasn't anyone else. She'd never had kids and she was divorced.' She felt a flicker of fear again. She leaned against the arm of the sofa, casually covering her mouth so there were no telltale signs visible. But eyes, she thought, the eyes tell. She could feel the older detective staring at her.

'Is that it?' she said brightly. 'Have I answered all your questions?'

'Not quite,' Pedersen said, taking out his notebook. 'I'd like to talk with your sister Jane's husband.'

For a moment she went blank. 'Oh, Jane's husband. I'm afraid he's dead. You know,' she went on hastily to cover her confusion, 'I find all this discussion of Jane very disturbing. I don't understand what it has to do with anything.'

He put his notebook in his pocket. She had moved him away from the topic of dead husbands. 'It's a link,' he said. 'A link with Eugénie.'

'A link with that bag lady? But what sort of link? I don't understand.'

'If Eugénie knew, say, that your sister had been assisted to her death, she'd have had excellent material for blackmail. As a blackmailer, she'd be in line for becoming a murder victim herself.'

'But that's ridiculous!' The words burst from her. 'I never heard anything so far-fetched. Jane killed herself. She was *depressed*. Besides, how would that explain Ann's death?' She was close to tears, the last thing she wanted in their presence.

'We can't answer that,' Tate said softly. 'That's what we need to know.'

'Well—' she stood up—'*I'm* not going to be able to tell you. If you don't need me any longer, I have an appointment—' she glanced at her watch—'in fifteen minutes.'

Both men got up. 'Think about it, Mrs Brennan. You never received a blackmail letter, I gather.'

'I told you I didn't. If I had, I suppose that would make

me a murderer.' She laughed uncertainly. 'I'll think about it, but I doubt that any wonderful new insights will come to me. You're the ones who are supposed to know how to find out about these things. I'd think—' She left the sentence unfinished.

At the door she glanced again at Tate. He was a pleasant young man, not too young, probably only a few years younger than she. And surprisingly articulate for a policeman. Maybe when things were cleared up and Lew was out of the picture, she'd ask him by for a drink. She sighed. If her husband wasn't back.

And where in hell *was* he? There was something ominous in his not having called. No one at work had heard from him, either. Had he thrown in the towel and gone off to an island somewhere with his latest woman? The idea of him, formal and businesslike as he appeared to the world, lying on some tropical beach in a bikini made her want to laugh, but the laugh caught in her throat.

Shaking, she sank into a chair and took out another cigarette. She was glad she had no appointments until her dinner engagement with Lewis.

CHAPTER 26

At first he didn't recognize her. When was it he had last seen her, ten, twelve years, more? He was fifty-eight so she must be close to that, but her dark hair had become grey, completely grey. And the waist he remembered clasped by bright belts was now markedly thickened. But she was still Martha, still wore a gipsylike South American-looking skirt and over her shoulder had draped a bright shawl.

And she greeted him as the old Martha had. Although, he thought, God knows she must be noticing the same things about me. Before leaving the house he had examined himself in the mirror and been pleased, but now, seeing himself through her eyes, he recalled that he had to pull back his shoulders and draw up his head to disguise the slight softness beneath his chin. But she greeted him in the old way, taking his hands and drawing him into the house, then standing on tiptoe and kissing him on the mouth.

For a moment he was startled, then she became familiar again. 'Martha,' he said, 'I've thought of you so often. I should have called months ago.'

She laughed. He remembered he had particularly liked her laugh. 'Well, we're together now. Will you have a drink or do we have a reservation for right this minute?'

'We have a reservation for eight. There's time for a drink.' He looked around the room. She had lived in this house before she was married, but it was changed. She followed his eyes. 'Holman had things, too. We combined them,' she said. 'I've grown used to it this way.' He followed her into the kitchen and surprised in himself a great sense of relief that it was unaltered from the way he remembered it. Making a move to mix the drinks, he checked himself. She had never accepted—or required—those little niceties he took for granted between men and women. Once, he remembered, she had let him mix drinks, standing watching him with a quizzical expression. When he had finished she had said, 'What was there about that you thought I couldn't do, Stanley? Lift the bottle?' He had been disconcerted and she amused. After that he hadn't volunteered. He was touched by a warm wave of pleasure at being with her once more, the person whose eccentricities and preferences he had once grown to love. How could they have quarrelled and given up all those years of companionship? But he had been a different person then, less sure, less established, less confident. Otherwise, he could never have let her go.

Settled opposite each other in the living-room, each studied the other's face. 'You look tried, Stanley,' she said. 'This business of Ann's death must have been a terrible strain.'

A flicker of anxiety went through him and for a moment he longed to tell her just how upset, bereft, he had been, but he smiled. 'I thought when I dressed today that I looked quite handsome. Hale.' She relaxed him, made it possible for him to be safely humorous. Always with his family, his attempts at humour had fallen flat. As a result, he had become increasingly staid around them. A flare of anger was struck in him at the recollection of Kay's words the other evening, her saying he never *did* anything. 'But,' he said to Martha, more seriously, 'it has been hard. The service is this weekend. Sunday. Will you come?'

She looked confused. 'I? I never really knew Ann, Stanley. But of course if you want me to, if it would make you feel better . . .'

'It would, you know. I don't—have many people.' It was true. There would be friends of Ann's, friends of Roy's and Kay's, even friends of the children there, but none of his own. The last couple of years he had let himself become absorbed in the business to the exclusion of friendship, had become what they labelled these days a workaholic. Kay had been right, except for business lunches and the occasional lunch or dinner with Ann, he didn't do anything. Hadn't, that was. He needed Martha to make him whole again.

He decided to put the business of her husband behind them. 'Was your marriage happy, Martha?'

'It was. The last couple of years Holman wasn't well and he . . . lost his sense of humour, but until then it was good. He was a fine man.'

The appropriate expression. But he found himself pleased, and mentally chided himself for it, that her marriage hadn't been perfectly smooth.

'It should have been me,' he said. 'We should never have quarrelled.'

She smiled. 'We were behaving in a pretty human way. I think you'd been alone so long you were scared to be any other way, and I was pressing you. I wanted the comfort of marriage, even though it was too late for kids. At the time, our splitting up made a lot of sense for both of us.'

'Only because I was crazy.'

She laughed. 'Not crazy. Maybe short-sighted. At any rate, it's all water under the bridge now. No point in hashing it over, no point at all.'

Her acceptance of the situation disturbed him. He wanted at least some small expression of regret from her. He could see he was not going to get it.

He finished his drink. Hers had been short and she had already set her glass down. 'Let's go, then. Let's pretend it's fifteen years ago.'

But even to that she did not respond.

Roy was still coping with the boys. Attributing their lumpishness to grief might explain it to those outside the family, but he had seen them frequently enough in their young lives to know better. Odd that they were so different from Suzanne, who seemed to him brimming with enthusiasms, commitments, plans, flightiness—the complex of contrasts he'd expect of any normal young man or woman in his or her twenties. But the boys simply sat and looked decorative. It *must* be grief, he conceded, becoming more generous as he considered the abruptness and horror of Ann's death. His notion that they were apprehensive about him was ridiculous. Impossible.

At the moment they were animated, however; they were in disagreement about dinner. Roy had suggested a quiet restaurant where at this hour—close to eight—they could find a good meal with no wait. The boys had in mind a quasi-Irish pub they had spotted. Just as he had conceded the point, the twins changed their minds and decided the restaurant was the better idea. Hastily he agreed, but the brief sputter of disagreement, even anger, among them enlivened things for Roy. With a heartier and more affectionate manner than he could usually muster, he herded them out.

At The Glade, they descended by funicular. Then, just as they were entering the restaurant, Roy spotted Stan entering with a woman—by God, that woman he used to see. What was her name? Mary? Martha, that was it.

'What luck,' he said. 'The boys were saying they'd seen almost nothing of you! Let's take a table together.' By God, he thought, I don't give a damn if I mess up his evening, I've had these clods wished on me all week, he can do his bit. 'And Martha!' He shook her hand and turned to the boys. 'Let me introduce you to Ann's sons, Martha. Meredith and Ellery, and Jason. This is Mrs—' He recalled that she had married, but went blank on the name.

'Smithson,' she prompted. 'I'm delighted to meet you. I want to say how sorry I am about your mother. I'll be at the service.'

That they turned to her with relief did not escape Roy. They're as tired of me as I am of them, he thought with amusement. Maybe they're only clods with me.

Stanley was glaring at him. He'd expected that. 'We were planning to discuss some things for which we need privacy,' he began, but it was too late. A waiter had been informed by Meredith that it was a party of six and they were being ushered to a table, Martha ahead surrounded by the boys. 'What's the big idea?' Stan managed between tight lips.

'I've had them all week, you take them on for a couple of hours.' Roy walked ahead and joined the group seating itself.

They were already deep in talk. Meredith, who had barely spoken to his uncle once the memorial service plans had been made, was excitedly describing the first year of law school. 'You wouldn't believe what being on law review means, it's everybody's goal. It makes the difference between a seventy-five-thousand-dollar a year job to start and one that begins at forty. Or less.'

'Forty sounds pretty good to me,' Martha commented. She turned to Ellery. 'You're in law, too?'

'We're dissimilar twins,' Ellery said, to Roy's amazement

attempting a joke. 'No, Jay and I are working on MBAs.' He smiled. 'I'm a year ahead of Jason, though.'

'He boasts a lot,' Jason explained. 'But he is more committed to the programme than I am,' he added.

Martha raised her eyebrows. 'Are you reconsidering, then?'

'Not really. It was just a thought.'

'Well, don't follow through on it,' Stanley put in. He seemed to have resigned himself, if grudgingly, to the company of his nephews. 'I changed my mind several times and, believe me, it set me back years.'

Jason and Ellery looked at their uncle with interest, as though he had suddenly become a valid human being to them. 'What—' Jason began, but the waiter's appearance stemmed conversation.

'You know,' Martha said, after their orders had been taken, 'I saw you all once when you were little. You won't remember, I think you were barely out of elementary school, but Stanley and I dropped by to pick up something from your mother. There was a little girl, too—your sister? Where is she tonight?'

Roy glanced guiltily at the boys. 'I never thought to call her. Did it occur to any of you?'

'Crossed my mind,' said Ellery, 'but when we asked her last time, she was going somewhere with Ollie.'

'Ollie. That rings a bell.' Martha turned to Stanley.

'Ann's friend. Her suitor for years.' Roy glanced at him. He could see Stan wished they wouldn't keep bringing up Ann. It must have been hell on Stan, finding her that way.

He noted the relief on Stanley's face as the waiter, loaded tray in hand, headed their way with the first course.

Kay Brennan and Lewis Mawson had considered The Glade but decided in favour of a restaurant seated high on a hill behind one of the town's hospitals.

'You like the proximity of a hospital,' Kay remarked as

they waited for their drinks. 'Aren't there supposed to be people who feel safer in an institutional environment?'

'There are. You're getting too wise since your acquaintance with me.' He said it good-naturedly, but she could see that he was annoyed. 'I'm *not* one,' he added. 'Ah.' He picked up the Bloody Mary that had just been brought.

'That looks a little gory for this particular week,' Kay commented, glancing at his glass.

Lewis set down his glass with a little crack. 'Are you planning to needle me all evening?'

'No.' She forced herself to relax. 'Sorry. I wasn't trying to needle you, I guess I was just expressing my preoccupations. Did you have a ghastly day?'

'Not ghastly, but not good. I didn't exactly savour that visit from the fucking police.'

'Oh yes, I forgot that. They did come by, just as you said they would. Like clockwork. Predictable.'

He leaned towards her, frowning. 'What did they ask you?'

'Whether you knew the family, particularly Ann. And whether you had any reason to be afraid of the family. I think that was it.'

'Afraid? What did you say?'

'I said, "Afraid of what?"'

'And?'

'They seemed to think you knew something about Ann's death. Or—' she raised her eyes and looked at him with calculation—'Jane's death.'

'What? Oh, Jesus—' He had upset his drink. 'I'm amazed they didn't also ask if I killed Eugénie. You didn't—?'

After the waiter had mopped up and brought another drink, Lewis went on, his voice more controlled. 'What do they know about Jane's death?'

'That's the question. What do they know?'

'Well, didn't they give any hint? Christ!'

'They know she didn't die of cancer.'

'You told them?'

'I told them she drowned herself, but that the official version was cancer.'

'They must know something, they wouldn't be bringing up this stuff otherwise. Fuck it.'

'I don't see why *you're* so upset. I should be the one.'

'I'm upset *for* you. That was it?'

'Not quite. They asked if there had ever been a suggestion of foul play, I think that's the way they put it, in Jane's death.'

They stared at each other, silent.

'And,' Kay went on after a minute, 'whether there was a will.'

'And who the beneficiaries were.'

'Yes.'

'He thought she was killed—and killed for her money, is that what he was hinting?'

Kay was suddenly irritable. 'Who knows what he thought? I told him we inherited. It wasn't much, God knows, the hospital bills had eaten up a good deal of it.'

'Was it enough to commit murder over?'

'I put him off that idea. At least I think I did. But they think something's wrong.'

'You know, Kay—'

'I know what's coming. You don't want to see me till this thing is cleared up.' Her jaw was set.

'It's just—it's just not good for me to be associated—so closely associated, that is—with a murder. That's the only reason. It's nothing to do with you. You know how I feel about you.'

'Lewis, you're just an old-fashioned courtly gentleman, aren't you? Throw the little girl to the wolves and save your own skin.'

'I'm a physician, for Christ's sake. And a psychiatrist. I can't *afford* this, visits from the police, inquiries into my relationship with the family. How the hell did they even find out we were seeing each other?'

'Who knows? We aren't secretive about it. Anybody could have seen us.'

'It's somebody at the hospital. I've taken you to a couple of parties. They hate me.'

'They? Who is *they*? God, you sound paranoid.'

'Never mind. And let me deal out the psychiatric jargon, if anybody does. At least I'm qualified.' His face become cold. 'I'm not going to see you till this is over, Kay.'

'And if I decide to share with the police some of your little preferences? And maybe that episode with Eugénie? That should put you right in line as a murder suspect.'

He had paled. 'You wouldn't do that. You have as much at stake as I.'

'I wouldn't absolutely count on it, Lewis. Here comes the waiter. Shall we order?'

At work in the museum the next morning, Roy indulged in a rare moment of introspection. He gave the impression of being a contemplative man, he was sure, but in fact he was not. As a boy, aware of differences between himself and other boys, he had gone through a long period of examining his motives, but the process had proved too painful to continue. In recent years he had developed a mode of managing his life that satisfied him; he dealt with the world on what he supposed would be regarded as a superficial basis. He allowed himself deep pleasure in things æsthetic—the smooth surface of a seashell, the explosion of colour in an abstract painting, a richly textured fabric, a piece of music. But aside from that, he functioned in terms of action without analysis. And when it came to human relationships, he held himself slightly apart. He had easy friendships with people he might never see again and not feel a sense of loss, he took lovers who satisfied his body's needs, but he kept his distance emotionally. This all went towards creating the bland, easy manner that he knew was assumed to be paired with thoughtfulness.

But today he wondered. Last night Stan had been upset

at mention of Ann. Shouldn't he too be feeling *something*? The only emotion of which he had been aware in the past week was irritation with the boys. He had gone through the motions, comforting Kay and remaining steady in the face of Stan's hysterics over the family image the other night, but he hadn't *felt* anything. What did that make him, some sort of conscienceless sociopath? Or was he in shock? He had heard that people confronted by a dreadful event sometimes remained numb, unfeeling, for days, even weeks afterwards. The thing that made him suspect that this wasn't the case was the familiarity of his absence of feeling. It wasn't stunned or unnatural, it was usual.

He sighed as he lifted a painting to try it against the newly grey-green wall. Certainly this state of mind was better than going to pieces over the events of the past few days. Even Kay and Stan hadn't done that. Maybe they felt no more than he, it was possible. Maybe no one felt anything when such things happened; perhaps they just pretended they did.

Somehow that thought eased his mind. Probably that was it. This business of feeling was highly overrated. Everyone was back at work, back to the business of living his life. Even Sue, who had seemed most affected, had gone to a class, he understood. Once the service was over, they could return to normal again. Death happened. Life meanwhile, as Stan had pointed out, must go on.

Yes, he decided, the painting was right in that spot. He relaxed into pleasure at the thought that all the choices for this show were his to make.

CHAPTER 27

The phone call from Jedediah Martin came just as Pedersen arrived at his office the next morning. For a moment the strange name didn't ring a bell. Then he remembered. 'Mr

Martin. Has something occurred to you?'

'You know, it has. I thought about all your questions, about your asking if Ann was afraid of anything or anyone. I remembered a letter she got.'

Pedersen was instantly alert. 'Yes?'

'I don't know what was in it, I didn't read it or anything. But a couple of weeks before she died, we were having dinner one evening and she said, "Jed, I received a terribly disturbing letter this morning." I said, "What was that?" or "What sort of letter?" something of that sort. Then she smiled, it was a rather forced smile, and she said, "No, I'd better think about it before I discuss it with you." She changed the subject and never referred to it again. Funny I didn't remember when you came in to talk to me.'

It was funny. Pedersen said, 'That was all? She didn't say who it came from or hint at why it was disturbing?'

'No. In fact, she was so completely herself for the rest of the evening that it went right out of my head. I never thought about it till now. If I thought anything at all when she said that, it was that one of her sons was in some sort of trouble with grades, something of that sort. It may have been that, it's just that with the . . . events of the last few days, it occurs to me that it may be something related to them.'

Probably the man's explanation was an honest one; a casual remark he interpreted as school trouble might easily not remain in the memory. He thanked Martin, told him if anything further occurred to him to call, and hung up.

It certainly sounded like the blackmail letter. Yet if it accused her or some other family member of murder, would she even have considered discussing it with a younger man with whom she had a casual, if friendly, relationship? Odd, unless it was like the confidence to the airline seatmate, told to someone who mattered so little one could confide freely. But if he could take them at their words, none of the other family members had received such a letter, and surely they would have mentioned it if they had known Ann had got one. Unless, of course, it was the one accused of murder whom she had told.

With whom would she have discussed such a letter? Would there have been anyone sufficiently in her confidence? Suzanne, her daughter? No. Surely she wouldn't have burdened her youngest child with upsetting information. Oliver Winter, her lover? If she had talked to anyone outside the family, it would likely have been her Ollie, who had known the family fortunes for years and might even have been able to advise her.

Pedersen remembered the man's anger. How could he approach him? He buzzed Tate.

'Trick him,' Tate said, standing at the window.

'Trick him? What do you mean?'

'Let him think you've found the letter among Ann Koppleman's things.'

'Hmm.' Pedersen dumped the worry beads on the desk. 'It's an idea. If he actually did see the letter, he'd try to explain it.'

'And probably inadvertently tell us a lot about it in the process.'

'I think this time I'll ask him to come in. Put him on the defensive, he's too sure of himself on home ground. Of course, he may refuse. He'd be within his rights and he seems very much aware of his rights.'

'You may end up with another complaint to Harbison.'

'I may. Nothing I can do about that.' He glanced at the office clock. 'I'm going to try him now before he gets out of the house.'

Oliver Winter seemed to have undergone a change of heart. Oh, Detective Pedersen worked on Saturday, too? Yes, it was convenient for him to stop by headquarters; he'd be happy to help Detective-Sergeant Pedersen in any way he could; he was pleased the investigation was moving ahead. Pedersen hung up, puzzled.

'What the hell's come over him? Suddenly he's all co-operation.'

'Maybe somebody in the family got to him, convinced him that making waves isn't the way to go.'

'Maybe. He'll be here in half an hour. You stick around, Ron, you see if *you* can size this guy up. I found him, shall we say, enigmatic?'

Ron Tate laughed. 'That'll be the day, when I can size up somebody you haven't figured out.' He removed his glasses. 'What else do we have to go on? This case gets complicateder and complicateder, as Alice would have said, if she had.'

'Mawson. I keep coming back to Mawson. His involvement with the family and with the hospital. And the thing that we don't know about him that's bothering him. Obviously the major candidates for murder, especially of Eugénie, are family members, but I don't see them wiping out both the blackmailer and the blackmail victim.'

Tate finished polishing his glasses and put them back on. 'Do you see this Jedediah person doing it?'

'No, his alibi's rock-solid. But Mawson's an unknown quantity. So's Oliver Winter.'

Oliver Winter arrived at precisely the moment he had said he would come. Dressed as he was in an impeccably tailored suit, white shirt, black tie, he was so unlike the usual visitor to the office as to seem remarkable. It occurred to Pedersen, not for the first time, that he always took particular notice of men in suits and ties in this town, they were so rare.

Pedersen introduced Tate.

Seated, Winter smiled agreeably. 'Now what can I tell you, gentlemen?' The mockery was still there, if faint, in his voice.

'We want to talk to you about a letter Ann Koppleman received.'

A quiver of some emotion—fear?—touched his face. But he said calmly, 'A letter?'

'Yes, a letter that was intended to be very disturbing to her.'

'And undoubtedly was,' Tate added.

'What did the letter say?' Winter remained in the same relaxed posture as when he had seated himself.

'It gave her information. We think you know what it said, Mr Winter. And from whom it came.' Pedersen slid open his shallow middle desk drawer and glanced into it, then closed it.

Winter adjusted his tie. 'It was written by some crank, just to upset her.'

'What in the letter made you think that?'

'Obviously it was untrue. Completely untrue. That's what made me think it.'

'What accusations—' Although he did not know why, the moment he said the word he realized he had made a mistake. 'What things in the letter were untrue?'

Winter's eyes had narrowed. 'You haven't read that letter, have you? You just know she received one.'

'But you have, Mr Winter. It would further our investigation if you were to tell us what parts of that letter struck you as untrue.'

'Why should I? Why should I do anything to sully Ann's name?'

The old-fashioned word startled Pedersen. '*Sully* her name?'

'This is what you police call a fishing expedition. She did receive a disturbing letter. I did see it. That's all I'm going to tell you. It was filled with untruths intended to hurt and upset her, even exploit her. But I am not going to repeat them to you.'

Pedersen leaned forward. 'You realize that the person who wrote that letter may have been a real threat to Mrs Koppleman.' As he said it, he thought: Not if it was Eugénie. At least, not a threat of death.

Winter appeared about to rise. 'Is there anything else?'

Pedersen pursued his point. 'You don't care that the person who wrote the letter was a threat to Ann Koppleman?'

'Of course I care! I simply don't believe it. If I'm forced in court to discuss the letter, I will. I won't do it voluntarily.' He paused as though considering. 'I am not being unco-operative, Detective. I honestly am convinced that the letter was from a crank, someone who envied Ann or her family and had decided to be malicious. If I thought it had any direct bearing on her death, I'd tell you every word in it. It doesn't. I believe that.' He walked to the door. 'I'm sorry to frustrate you.' He sounded as though he actually were sorry. 'I'll go along now.'

'One moment. Will you at least tell us who signed the letter?'

Winter put one hand on the doorknob. 'If I told you that, I might as well tell you what was in the letter.' He opened the door and was gone.

'Well,' said Pedersen. 'It can't have been signed with Eugénie's name or he'd have tied her in with Ann's death. The other day when I talked to him, he was convinced there was no connection between the two deaths or that Ann would have had anything to do with a bag lady. So who signed it?'

'Maybe she signed it with a phrase.'

' "Out to get you"?'

Tate laughed. 'No. Something descriptive. "One who knows". Something like that.'

'Would telling us have given away the whole show?'

'If it was a phrase, it could have been extremely descriptive. "One who knows you committed murder," for instance.'

'That could be. The other thing is, did you notice the word that gave away that we hadn't read the letter?'

'No. What was it?'

'Accusations. When I started to say, "What accusations—" Winter immediately knew I hadn't read the letter.'

'That means—'

'Yes. There were no accusations in the letter.'

'Then it wasn't an accusation of murder, the way you thought.'

'You know, Ron,' Pedersen said, taking a bag of peanuts from his desk drawer, 'we may have to rethink this whole thing.'

'If that letter didn't contain threats, what did it contain? If it didn't contain accusations—' Pedersen rubbed his eyes. They had been discussing the case for an hour and they had arrived back at the main question.

'Did it occur to you that the letter might have had nothing at all to do with Jane Potter's death?'

Pedersen groaned. 'Since an hour ago it's occurred to me.'

'The one thing we do know,' Tate said, 'is whom Eugénie sent the letter to. Ann.'

'We don't know that, we assume it. All we *know* is that Eugénie wrote a mysterious letter and Ann received a mysterious letter.'

'Then you don't think—'

'Oh, I do think. I just don't *know*.'

'It's a bitch, this case, isn't it?' Tate commented. 'Nothing fits. Everybody is involved with everybody else, but not a goddamned thing *fits*.'

'You're singularly gloomy about this, Ron. Look at the positive side of things. We're being challenged.' He sighed. 'In fact, you might say we're being stumped.'

'You might.' They looked at each other.

CHAPTER 28

Freda had proposed meeting for lunch after she finished at the Counselling Aid Centre. She arrived, on her face the satisfied, slightly introspective glaze Pedersen had come to anticipate after her meetings with other counsellors. Today, however, he had no humour about it. About anything, for that matter.

'This case,' he said after they had installed themselves at the outdoor café of Kettle House and ordered, 'is *impossible.*'

She looked surprised. 'Don't you always think that?'

'Jane Potter ties in there in some way and I haven't the first notion where,' he went on, ignoring her, 'and nobody's about to tell me, either.'

'You've tried Roy?'

'Roy?'

'That brother. Roy.'

'Why Roy?'

'I have an idea from what you've told me that he likes to be important.'

Pedersen sat back so the waitress could set his plate before him. 'Is this some notion you've gotten from counselling?'

She laughed. 'No. Just common sense.'

'What have I told you that led to that conclusion? *What?*'

'Oh, when you described them, he came across as someone who's always taken a back seat in that family.'

'I don't know. Sometimes I think I shouldn't discuss my cases with you, Freda.'

She began on her salad. 'It's just an idea. You're on edge today, Carl. It's not like you.'

'It's not, but this case is so damned frustrating. And every time I turn around, Harbison has another complaint about me. Maybe I need a vacation.'

'You always need a vacation, that's nothing new. I think if you just take it easy and go about things the way you usually do, without any fuss, you'll come up with the answers.' She reached across the table and touched his hand.

Pedersen could feel himself let go. 'You're good for me. Like medicine. A tonic,' he said.

She made a face. 'What a dreadful comparison. Can't I be good for you in some pleasanter way than medicine? You never take medicine, anyway.'

He laughed, his equilibrium mysteriously restored. 'Like a hike through a pine woods? Like a dip in the bay at noon in the dead of summer? Like sex in the morning? Is that better?'

She grinned. 'Much. Why don't you try Roy Potter? It can't do any harm.'

'I've just decided I will. I never belittle your intuitive powers.' At her expression, he added, 'Your common sense contributions, I mean.'

She raised her eyebrows. 'Now. Let's talk about me for a change.'

He found Roy at the museum. Alone in the large gallery, Roy Potter was shifting about paintings of a strange delicacy; Pedersen was struck by their simplicity. 'Mr Potter, frankly I'm stuck. I've come to you for help. Can you work and talk at the same time?'

'I can try. I'm not sure I can help you much.'

'I think so. You strike me as sensitive, aware of people and what makes them tick.' I'm slathering this on too thick, he thought, Freda's instinct about this man had better be right.

Apparently it was. Roy put down the painting he was holding and turned to Pedersen, a pleased expression on his face. 'I'll try to help. Let's sit down back there.' He led Pedersen to a bench behind a screen. 'Everybody's out of the building at the moment, we won't be bothered.'

'It's your sister Jane,' Pedersen said. He sensed an immediate tensing in the other man.

'Jane. She died ten years ago.'

'I know she did. This will seem strange to you, but I'd like you to tell me about her. You'd have been aware of the . . . facets of her personality, the things that made her different from the other members of the family. That's the sort of thing I need to know.'

'But *why*? She's been dead almost ten years.'

'Let's say—let's put my motives aside for a minute. Could you do that?'

'I suppose,' Potter said, grudging. 'Jane.' His face grew soft. 'Jane was the sensitive one in the family, not me. She was—how can I describe her? When we were little, Ann rescued lost kittens, but it was Jane who became . . . emotionally involved with them. She wasn't very sure of herself, Ann had a confidence that Jane never had, but Jane was intensely loyal to those people she—valued.' He looked up at the detective. 'You know, this is hard for me.'

'You were very attached to her?'

'She was two years older than I, Ann was three years younger. I was the middle child in the family. Jane sort of took care of me, she was always putting Band-Aids on my hurt knees and comforting me when she thought someone had treated me badly. She . . .' An odd expression crossed his face, as though he were experiencing an unfamiliar emotion. 'She was a good big sister. She had little quirks, like all of us—she liked secrets, I remember. She wasn't exactly secretive, but she did like secrets.'

'What about her as an adult? What happened with her marriage?'

'As an adult she was over-sensitive. Easily hurt. Then her husband left her and found someone else, that really hit hard.' Pedersen glanced away and when he looked back caught a look of calculation on Roy Potter's face. It passed. 'She went to pieces. Wept and wept and wept. Finally the family saw that it wasn't just a passing thing and persuaded her to consider hospitalizing herself. By this time she wasn't crying any more, but she was . . . immobilized. Just sitting. Or lying, all curled up. Not eating. It was very upsetting to all of us.'

'So she was persuaded.'

'Yes, but she didn't want anyone to know. I think she thought other people found her strange and she kept saying that we must pretend she was in the hospital for some ordinary illness.'

'And did you?'

'At first. Actually, at first we just didn't mention that she was hospitalized, but—'

'She had to go to Fernwood.'

'Yes. And after a while she saw a few friends.'

'And ultimately you did dismiss her illness as having been what one might call an ordinary one.'

'That was Kay's idea, I think. Or Ann's. They thought it might explain her being out of circulation for so long.'

'Then what?'

'What happened next couldn't have come at a worse time. She had been seeming better, we had talked to her about signing herself out. Then one weekend when all of us, *all* of us, were out of town, she did it. I think she waited for that chance.'

'All four of you away. That seems oddly coincidental.'

'I know. Ann and Kay had gone up to Mendocino for the weekend—both their husbands were tied up with meetings or were away, I've forgotten. And I visited a friend in Big Sur for the weekend. Stan was recovering from a broken love-affair and decided to take his boat out by himself. That's not a good practice, but he did it and slept on the boat for several days, just getting away, having a change of scene. By the time we returned, Jane had signed herself out and simply vanished.'

'And then?'

'We talked about going to the police, but we were afraid if she was just off someplace, recovering from the hospitalization as it were, she'd be furious. So we hired a private detective to try to find her. He found her.'

'Two weeks later.'

'Yes, but the thought was that she had died the day or within a day of getting out of the hospital.'

'You found her at the morgue?'

'Yes, the detective called us. He was pretty sure it was Jane, but he wanted us to identify her.'

'Was there any suggestion of foul play, Mr Potter?'

'You mean was she pushed, something like that?'

'Or strangled or knocked out?'

He looked shocked. 'No. The autopsy would have shown that, wouldn't it?'

'Yes. But was there any hint of that brought up?'

'No. Who could have done it? We were all away, if that's what you're hinting at. And she had been out of touch with everyone while she was in the hospital, even her closest friends. That thing about secrets I told you about, that was in full play while she was hospitalized.'

'I'm amazed that anyone could conceal such a secret for the better part of a year.'

'It was a little amazing. I suppose, to tell the truth, we weren't any of us exactly happy about having a member of the family under psychiatric care. We abetted her in her efforts to keep it quiet.' He sighed. 'It all seems like such a long time ago. I haven't thought about Jane in several years. I guess you block out things like that.'

'And you've received no communication, no letter, no phone call about her death in recent weeks?'

'No. You asked me that before. What is this all about, all this business about Jane?'

Pedersen looked at him thoughtfully. 'We're wondering if Eugénie, that's the bag lady who was murdered the same night as your sister Ann, somehow got wind that there was foul play in Jane's death. And was blackmailing a member of the family.' He thought: I persist in this notion, despite evidence. Ron's right about me, I get on a hobby-horse and ride it, even if it's going nowhere.

Roy Potter stood up abruptly. 'I never heard such nonsense.'

'Your sister Ann received a disturbing letter just before her death. Several people have told us.'

'That doesn't make sense. Why would both of them be killed then?'

Pedersen sighed. 'That's what catches us up every time.'

'And how could this bag lady get such information? She must have manufactured it.'

'She must have known about your sister Jane to manufacture it. And despite no signs of foul play, Jane *could* have been pushed off those rocks.' Of course, he thought, what I'm not telling this man is that Eugénie was a nurse and might well have known Jane. Or that this is all speculation, we don't know what the letter said.

Potter thrust his hands into his pockets. 'I don't buy it. Any of it. It sounds crazy. I think some maniac just bought a couple of knives and used them the same night.'

'That's odd, too, Mr Potter. It's almost as though he were directing us to see a connection between the murders—same knives, same price stickers on them. You can see what we're up against.'

Potter sat down as suddenly as he had stood. 'I do see. It's hard to understand. But so far as Jane is concerned . . .' He drew a hand across his eyes, a weary gesture. 'That was disturbing enough to go through, that whole business of her illness and death. We don't need to drag it all up again.'

'I don't know, Mr Potter, we may need to. One last thing, then I'll leave you to your pictures. They're—' he tried to find another word—'beautiful, those paintings. I think I'll come to your exhibit.' And bring Freda, he thought. She'll love them.

'Yes? The one thing?'

'What was your sister Jane's married name?'

A strangely resistant expression seized Roy Potter's face. 'What does that have to do with anything? The man's dead now.'

'I'd still like to know.' Now that it occurred to him, several family members had skirted answering this question.

Or had he not asked the question this directly? He couldn't remember. 'The name?'

There was a moment of silence. Then, in a low voice, Roy Potter said, 'Her name was Jane Koppleman.'

'Koppleman? You mean—?'

'Yes, Ernest left Jane in order to marry Ann.'

CHAPTER 29

This time, Stanley decided, nothing was going to spoil his evening with Martha. He would ask her to dinner at his house, broil a steak for her. She could help with the salad and he'd lay in some good wine and buy a dessert, French pastry perhaps. He'd even remember to stop off at the good bakery, though it was off the beaten track for him and he always had to line up and take a number. Their bread almost made it worthwhile.

But he might have known: Martha would have no part of it. 'Come to me,' she said; her old-fashioned phrasing was one of the things that endeared her to him. 'I'll make a roast, rare, the way you like it. You can bring dessert if you want.' At any rate, at her house they would not be interrupted any more than at his. He was elated all day.

Shortly before he was to leave work, the phone call came. It was that detective again, Pedersen; he was becoming a real nuisance. 'Yes?' Stanley said, 'I have another call waiting, can we make it quick?' That was a lie, but somehow he felt the evening to which he was so looking forward was fragile and would be spoiled if he lingered too long on the phone with the detective.

Pedersen's voice came clearly over the wire, startling Stanley with its words. 'Tell me, Mr Potter, what relationship did Ernest Koppleman have with your sister Jane after their divorce? Did he pay her hospital bills?'

'What?' For a moment Stanley couldn't get his bearings.

'Who told you about that?' He was outraged that someone in the family would have bandied about, that was the way he thought of it, Ann and Jane's private affairs. 'Who?'

'Your brother, but reluctantly, you may be sure.'

'Damn Roy! That old business! Why would you want to know about it, anyway?' He was having trouble controlling his voice. The fiction of the waiting phone call was forgotten.

'We have reasons. Did your brother-in-law pay Jane's bills?'

'Yes, most of them. That whole affair, the business of his marrying Ann after the divorce, was unfortunate, none of us liked it. But it happened and we lived with it. Is *that* going to be passed along to the press, I suppose?' His evening was ruined, he knew. He could never regain the sense of well-being that had pervaded his day.

'I don't see why the press should know anything about it unless, of course, it proves particularly relevant. What was the timing—did your sister Jane know about her former husband's involvement with Ann before the actual marriage took place?'

He supposed he had no choice but to answer. 'No. It was that that caused her depression, we thought, discovering it wasn't just some anonymous woman, but her sister that he'd been interested in all along. *Must* we go into all this?'

'I'm afraid we must. So there was the separation, the divorce and then this sudden shock, the marriage to her sister. That must have produced a lot of guilt in Ann, especially when her sister broke down.'

'I'm sure Ann felt bad about it. She didn't *plan* it, after all. She didn't do it to Jane on purpose.'

'I see.' There was a pause, no doubt while Pedersen thought up some other embarrassing question. He had. 'There wasn't any particular rivalry between the sisters, then?'

'No! Ernest comforted Ann after her husband's death—she was pretty broken up and he came around and did little things for her, helped her with finances and settling the estate, and one thing apparently led to another. I'm sure neither of them intended it. I just don't understand all this interest in Jane. She died almost ten years ago, why are you bringing her into things?' Stanley suddenly felt tired, as though the evening's plans were beyond his energies. How could he be pleasant and relaxed with Martha after this interrogation? He sighed deeply.

Pedersen must have heard him. 'I know all this is upsetting to the family. To you. We think the link between Eugénie, the bag lady, and your sister Ann may be Jane. We think Eugénie found out something about Jane's death and was trying to blackmail your sister Ann. We haven't fitted things together properly but that's the reason for the interest in Jane.'

'You found a blackmail letter?'

'No, we're hypothesizing. And we may be wrong, but we have to pursue this line till we're sure we're wrong, if we are.'

'You think there was something . . . suspect about Jane's death?'

'There could be. She could have been pushed off those rocks.'

'But you mean that some person—that Ann—?' He could hear that his voice was faint.

'Someone. We're not making any assumptions yet about who did the pushing.'

'I—Stanley felt he had handled all he could handle. God knew what bombshell the man was about to unleash next. He remembered. 'That other phone call. I have to go. Is that it?'

'That answers my questions. Thank you for your time, Mr Potter.' Pedersen rang off.

Stanley sat looking at the phone as though it had spat venom. If what Pedersen said was true, the police thought Ann had pushed Jane off the rocks. Surely they wouldn't think she'd do such a thing merely because she felt guilty over marrying Ernest? And how did they account for Ann's death, if they believed that? They were hopelessly muddled, chasing down a wrong trail, but Pedersen's suggestions had made him uneasy, uncertain. That Roy. Roiling the waters as usual, although probably he had been on the spot exactly as he, Stanley, had when Pedersen asked him about the relationship.

He began to gather up papers on his desk, preparatory to leaving. He wished the whole thing were behind him, not poisoning a day like this, one which had started out so auspiciously. Imagine suspecting Ann, gentle Ann who rescued kittens.

Well, he decided, he might as well leave, stop off to pick up dessert, go on to Martha's, down a couple of drinks and try to put behind him Pedersen's intrusion into his happiness. Easier, he thought as he closed the door to his office, said than done.

But when he arrived the house had such a jaunty air that he could not remain depressed. Martha had laid a fire which blazed brightly and set a table before it with coloured pottery and lighted candles. He recalled that she had always struck the right note of intimacy, or formality if the occasion called for it, when she entertained. Looking around the warm room, he thought: Kay's right, my living-room does look like a public lounge.

He dropped the bakery box on the kitchen counter and seated himself on a stool to watch her. She was rinsing spinach leaves and slicing a red pepper and mushrooms and papery onion rings into a salad bowl, her hands deft and graceful.

She glanced up. 'You look exhausted. Why don't you pour yourself a drink?'

Gratefully he poured himself a double bourbon, splashing a little water into it. 'I am tired,' he admitted. 'Martha, you don't know what it means to come here at the end of a day.' He took a gulp of his drink and, whether from the whisky itself or the prospect of its effects, felt himself relax. 'You're a *soothing* woman. You remind me of Ann.'

He hadn't meant to say that; to his ears, his voice sounded choked.

She smiled and poked a strip of red pepper at his mouth. 'And you're a sweet man to say so.' Her eyes were on his face. 'You miss her.'

He could not answer.

The dinner was delicious. Martha was a good cook; he could see how she had come by the extra roundness in her face and at her waistline; meals like this every night would threaten his trimness, he knew. But—a warm wave of feeling washed over him—how it would be to come home every night to a dinner like this! To Martha. For the first time since Ann's death he was drained of tension. He even considered telling Martha of his conversation with Pedersen, but he abandoned the idea. That would intrude the whole matter of the murder into their evening. What he needed tonight was to escape it.

Over coffee, he apologized. 'I'm sorry about Roy and the boys wishing themselves on us at dinner last night,' he said. 'Nothing I could do. I guess being paternal is difficult for Roy, he's had it with the three of them.'

'I didn't mind, I enjoyed meeting them. Your nephews seem so excited over their work.'

Stanley laughed. 'When we were leaving, Roy told me they hadn't shown a spark of interest in what they're doing until you showed up. You coaxed it out of them.'

'Didn't take much coaxing. The service is tomorrow, isn't it? I suppose after that they'll be going back.'

'Yes, and Roy can cease being on his good behaviour.'

'His good behaviour?'

'Ignore that, I shouldn't have said it. You've met Kay, haven't you?'

'A couple of times when we were all younger—she was in her thirties then, I think. Did they have children?'

'No.' Stanley was surprised at the question. 'Was she talking about having any? If so, you must have drawn her out, too, she's never expressed the least interest in parenthood in my presence.'

'I don't think she said anything. It just seemed to me that a married woman that age would be thinking of it, if she were ever going to.'

'You regret not having had kids, don't you, Martha?'

She met his eyes. 'I'd like to have had them. I've survived the loss.'

'Do you blame me? Keeping you hoping so long and then not coming through?'

'I never thought of it that way. I was capable of making choices. I chose you.'

'What about now, Martha? Would you choose me again?' He reached across the table for her hand.

After a moment she withdrew it. 'I don't know, Stanley. It's something I've thought about since you phoned.'

A sensation of foreboding gripped him. 'You decided something?'

'No.' She smiled. 'It's a little soon, isn't it? I haven't decided anything at all. Let's just take it a day at a time and see what we feel. Doesn't that make sense?'

'Yes, but I haven't the slightest desire to be sensible about you.'

Her laughter lightened the moment. 'Have some of this wickedly rich pastry, then. The sensible thing would be to ignore it.'

'You're avoiding the issue.'

'Not avoiding it, deferring it. No decisions for a while, Stanley. Do have some of this pastry. I'll eat it if you leave it, and I can't afford it.'

Probably, he told himself as he helped himself to a napoleon oozing with custard, she's right. We should take it a day at a time. But for the first time in his life, he felt sure. He hoped there wouldn't be too many days to live through. This was one thing in his life he was not going to botch.

CHAPTER 30

'Where are we now with the case?' Freda asked. She was standing at the stove, heating a stew she had prepared earlier in the day.

Pedersen raised his eyebrows. 'Where are *we*?'

'Where are *you*, then?' She grinned. 'You're so possessive about some things.'

He laughed. 'I'd gladly give this case away. No, that's not true. I've become fascinated with all the interrelationships. Everybody is something to someone else, but no pattern emerges from the connections.'

'What's the latest?' The stew's fragrance filled the kitchen. Freda's face was rosy from the heat.

He joined her at the stove. 'That smells wonderful. How about a taste? I'm ravenous.'

She offered him the spoon filled with chunks of vegetable and beef. 'I'm hungry, too. It's beginning to feel like fall. So, what's new in the case?'

'You won't believe it. Jane Potter was married to Ernest Koppleman before he married Ann.'

Freda stopped stirring. 'She *was*? You mean her sister swiped her husband?'

'For a lady who prides herself on her feminism, that's a pretty old-fashioned way of putting it, but it's the fact.'

'Had it been going on all the while?'

'I gather it happened after she lost her husband, her first one. Her brother-in-law became very helpful, settling the estate and all. Funny she didn't turn to her old friend Ollie.'

Freda had recommenced stirring. 'Maybe she didn't want anyone outside the family to know what her husband had left her.'

'Maybe not. Anyway, it happened and Jane's depression followed their divorce and his remarriage. She must not have been a very stable person, it was clinical depression, not the usual blues a person feels after a divorce.'

Freda was indignant. 'I'm sure most people feel more than "blues". *I'd* go into a real depression if you left me and married my sister.'

Pedersen grimaced. 'Please. Make it someone other than your sister. But there's not a chance you'd go into a depression. You'd find yourself someone new on the first corner you came to. You're not the sort of woman to pine away for any man.'

She turned to face him, spattering gravy on the floor. 'What do you mean? I'm unfeeling?'

'Not unfeeling.' He reached for a paper towel. 'Just too vital to be alone for long.'

'It's not easy for a woman in her fifties to find a man, you know.'

'You'd find one.'

'Why do you assume I'd want one? You know, Carl—' her face was thoughtful—'I think you're wrong. I think if something happened to us, if you died or we were divorced, I'd live alone. Or with another woman. I'd stop worrying about dinner being on time. I'd eat when I wanted to and sleep when I wanted to and stay up all night reading or listening to jazz if I felt like it. I'd travel and—don't look so stricken. I prefer it *this* way. I just don't think I'd do it again.'

'You sound so . . . enthusiastic. As though you can't wait to try a life like that.'

She slid the stew pot off the burner, set it aside and came over to him. 'There's absolutely nothing like a Significant Other and I know it. But I don't think you'd be easy to replace. It would be a better life than just marrying someone to get married, wouldn't it?'

He kissed her. 'At least you can talk about it. I can't *think* about your not being here. I'm the one who'd go to pieces.'

She shook her head. 'You always say that. You wouldn't. You'd find someone else within a year and live happily ever after. Men need women more. Don't smile, they do. Look at any widower, they can't wait to get themselves married again.'

'What are you working from, a sampling of two?

'No. I can read. I've read things. Men can't understand a woman's enthusiasm for a life alone. You've been free in a different way from us, especially those of us who stayed home with kids. The idea of not having to adapt to anybody else's needs or schedules sounds so *restful*.' After a moment, she added meditatively, 'Actually, it's probably pretty lonely.'

Pedersen crossed to the other side of the room. 'Don't let's discuss it. It bothers me to talk about it.'

'Then—' she returned to the stove and began ladling stew into heavy white bowls—'you understand some of what Jane felt when her husband left her, why it wasn't just the "blues".' She carried the bowls to the table. 'It must have been hell, seeing him practically next door with her sister. God! She must have wanted to kill him.'

'She probably did. And he probably wanted to murder her for making him feel so guilty.' He stopped. 'Maybe that's what happened. Maybe Ernest murdered her.'

Freda slid the salad bowl from a refrigerator shelf and brought it to the table. 'That's everything. You'd better forget the case for a while, it'll interfere with your digestion.'

He reached for a thick slice of dark bread. 'Nothing will interfere with this meal.' He picked up his fork. 'But I wonder. It doesn't explain anything, though. I guess that's one blind alley I won't chase down.' He took a first forkful of stew. 'Tomorrow is the service for Ann Koppleman.' After a while he added, 'This stew is *marvellous*.'

'Well, of course,' said Freda.

The attendance was surprisingly small. An announcement of the service had appeared the evening before and firmly specified that it was being held for 'family and close friends only'; either Ann's friends had been unable to determine what constituted closeness or her close friends had been few. Held in the town's Universalist Church, a little grey-painted building of no particular pretension located near the centre of town, the service, while personal, was not a true memorial service. The young minister obviously knew Ann well; he spoke of her work with Marigold House and the hospital and even of her dedication to the University's Garden Project, in each case citing specific incidents that demonstrated her selflessness in giving. At one point he seemed about to cry. When he finished speaking, a quartet played briefly. There were no eulogies or tributes from others.

Pedersen was surprised. He had the impression the whole thing was being got over with as quickly and unobtrusively as possible, as though there were some shame in Ann's having been murdered. Nonetheless, the family seemed deeply moved. At one point Stanley openly wept; throughout the service Kay crushed a handkerchief to her mouth, above which her eyes brimmed; Roy's features bore a mournful cast that altered his face's contours. The boys sat stolidly, eyes straight ahead, obviously keeping a grip on themselves. Suzanne quietly sobbed. Pedersen was touched.

But Oliver Winter, one of the few non-family members recognizable to Pedersen, was the most interesting. His face bore an expression of disdain throughout. Several times Pedersen glanced his way; the expression was unrelenting. Immediately the service was over, he rose from where he sat apart from the others and left without a word, even to Suzanne.

Pedersen hesitated a second, then followed him out. Winter was unlocking a black Mercedes as Pedersen approached; he jumped slightly when the detective spoke.

'Affecting service, Mr Winter, didn't you think?'

'I dislike this sort of thing myself,' Winter replied, straightening and facing Pedersen.

'Oh? Why is that?'

'It's too complex to explain to you.' The subtle emphasis on the word *you* was not lost on Pedersen.

'You don't feel there needs to be . . . closure after a death? A time to pay tribute? To, as it were, say goodbye?'

Winter looked off over Pedersen's shoulder. Pedersen was aware that the mourners were beginning to emerge from the building. 'I say goodbye in my own way.' Winter seemed to be reflecting to himself. 'There are many ways of saying goodbye.' He turned back to the car. 'I want to get out of here before I'm placed in the position of having to say things I don't mean to the family. Goodbye, Detective.' He climbed into his car, started the engine and roared off.

Odd, Pedersen thought, I'd have thought he's the one person who would be dedicated to the most conventional of funeral services. He turned back towards the church.

Roy Potter emerged from the church with a peculiar lightness of spirit. After the burial of the ashes in the family plot, it would be over. Although he still experienced a strange distance from real grief, he thought he had conducted himself well at the service. It was true that he could not weep on command as, apparently, Stanley could, but he had felt the sadness of a mourner. For a second he felt irritation that he could not weep or feel the loss as deeply as the others seemed to. But there it was again: seemed to. Who knew what they really felt? Or thought.

Stanley sought Martha as he turned to leave the church. She had come as he asked, and as he approached her, he realized she was crying. 'You seemed so upset, Stan,' she said, using his nickname as she seldom did. She smiled faintly, drying her eyes on a colourful handkerchief. 'It upset me, too.' He took her hand, touched. He noted that she had dressed with special restraint, given her wardrobe. She was really an extraordinary woman, a caring woman. For a moment he experienced a thrust of pain at the thought of the missed years and the children they might have had. He gripped her hand, hard.

Kay mopped her eyes and turned to leave the church, reaching beside her for Sue as they both stood up. The girl's hand was limp, as though she had been utterly enervated by grief. For a moment Kay felt an awful loneliness envelop her. She still had not had a word from her husband; he did not even know of Ann's death. Lewis seemed about to desert her completely and there was no one else at the moment. She turned and embraced Sue with a warmth unusual for her.

Pedersen, standing outside, watched them issue from the little grey building, wondering what they were feeling. As he moved towards the little family group that had stopped to one side of the door, receiving condolences, he reflected that they were a hard bunch to read.

CHAPTER 31

'I'd like it if it's here. I know it's only a Timex,' Rod MacMillan said, 'but it also happens to be the only watch I own. I must have left it upstairs when I went for my annual check-up Friday.'

The young woman behind the hospital's Lost and Found counter eyed him with doubt. 'I swear I've been through everything in the jewellery box twice. Couldn't you have left it somewhere else? Did you call upstairs?'

'Yes. They say they shoot everything down here the day they find it. Can't I look?'

She glanced around. 'Come on. I'm not supposed to let anyone back here, but since you work in the hospital, I guess it's OK.' She led him to a back room. 'Here.' She slid a box off a shelf. It appeared to be filled with pieces of costume jewellery.

'My God, *everyone* must be careless. What a collection.'

'I'll go back to the desk. You look through this, but you won't find it. There are a couple of wristwatches, but not yours.'

The assortment was fascinating. Gold predominated.

Rings, pins, watches, a bracelet, a chain and locket. He paused over the locket to see if it contained pictures. It did, of two children. Someone was really missing that. One watch was a Seiko. How could anyone be that careless? He picked up several unmatched earrings. Had the women left wearing single earrings? Obviously the girl was right; his watch wasn't among this assortment, although everything else was. Even, he picked it up, a wedding ring. That carried some significance, he thought with amusement. Had the woman taken it off and abandoned it with unconscious intent? He smiled and looked inside the ring. 'E/J forever,' it read. He put it down, then in a sudden moment of recollection he saw Eugénie's hand, quiet in her lap as she answered his questions. She had been wearing a wedding ring; he had especially noticed it, wondering why she hadn't long since pawned a piece of gold like that. He looked at the ring again. E/J? Eugénie/John? Eugénie/James? Eugénie/Jules? He picked it up, oddly excited. Could it possibly be Eugénie's ring?

'No watch,' he announced as he came out of the room. 'But I found something else.'

'No kidding. Something you lost?'

'No, but something I want to show the police.'

She looked shocked. 'The police?'

'In connection with that murder last week. This may have belonged to the murdered woman.' He held out the ring.

'I can't let you take something that belongs to someone else.' Her face crinkled with distress.

'Then hold it aside, someplace safe, till I phone the police to see if they're interested. Will you do that?'

'All right. I'll put it in an envelope and label it with your name. Will the police come right away?' Her face was anxious.

'I don't know, they may not come at all. But don't let anything happen to it. And thanks about my watch. If it turns up, call Social Work and leave a message for me, will you?'

Back in his office, he had Jerry Cohen paged.

Jerry remembered. 'That's right, she had a ring. When she told me she was married, she sort of waved her hand to show it to me. Gold, I think it was.'

'Yes, gold. I'm going to call Detective Pedersen and tell him about it. If it's hers, she might have left it on a bedside table or something.'

'Earlier. I'm sure they removed everything that was in the room the day she died. But you might as well tell the police, just in case. If it were hers, it might help them—'

'I know, identify her,' Rod broke in.

He could hear the amusement in Jerry's voice. 'Do you feel like a detective?'

He laughed. 'I do, it makes me want to start searching the hospital for clues. Anyway, sorry to bother you, but I wanted to tell someone. I'd better get through to the police before that girl in Lost and Found mislays it or something.'

Detective Pedersen was not in his office. The switchboard transferred the call to Detective Tate's office.

Tate sounded dubious. 'You think it's hers? All gold wedding rings look alike, don't they? And that E could be anybody.' He paused. 'Well, maybe I'll come by and take a look, I have to be over in that neighbourhood around noon anyway.'

Rod felt impelled to elaborate. 'It was coincidence, really. If I hadn't lost my watch, the ring could have lain there for months.'

'Then if it turns out to be hers, luck is on our side. But don't get your hopes up.' He still sounded unconvinced.

Rod MacMillan hung up, conscious that the papers on his desk needing his attention seemed singularly dull and uninteresting. He smiled to himself. Maybe he'd missed his calling.

*

Pedersen examined the ring doubtfully. He had just returned from a follow-up visit to Marigold House—Tate had made the first—and had confirmed his impression that no one having to do with that organization had the slightest connection with either murder. Tate had meanwhile picked up the ring.

'I suppose we could have the *Banner* run a photo,' Pedersen said.

'Enlarge the inscription,' Tate offered.

'Yes, if it was hers, maybe someone who knew her will recognize it. It might lead to our knowing who the hell she was.' He sat down wearily. 'Next time we have a service to attend, you take it, Ron. I almost didn't get up this morning.'

'Too bad she didn't put both her initials and both of his in the ring. That might have been enlightening,' Tate said.

'Not really.' Pedersen poked in his desk drawer. 'I'm sure I had some peanuts—oh, here they are.' He tore open the packet. 'Supposing it were Eugénie's, which it probably isn't, the ring tells us just one thing, the first initial of her husband. J, that could be Jonathan, Jeffrey, Joseph—the possibilities are endless. Endless. I suppose we should ask the *Banner* to do something with it, but we've had no response to her picture, why should we think we'll do better with this?'

'You do sound tired. Discouraged. That's—'

'I know. That's not like me.'

'Well, it isn't.'

'So my wife told me. I am discouraged. Usually at least we know whom we're dealing with. This business of her having no identity gets to me. We keep learning scraps of things, but none of it has helped us with *her*. I don't understand why someone hasn't come forth to say, "That looks like a woman I once knew," or "I went to school with a girl named Eugénie." Can she have changed that much?' He broke a peanut in half and examined it for the dwarf.

'Did you ever think that maybe people who might know her are uneasy about identifying themselves with a vagrant?'

'We'd give them anonymity. Maybe we haven't stressed

that enough. Tell the *Banner* when they take the ring over, will you? Tonight,' Pedersen went on, eating the halves of the peanut, 'I'm going to sit down with a sheet of paper and graph this case. Look at all the relationships and see if I can't come up with something.'

Tate smiled. 'When you turn to a paperwork solution, you must be desperate.'

'I am desperate. Don't you feel we must have enough at our fingertips to solve this, but that we're missing some obvious connection?'

'I'd—oh my God, I forgot. When I picked up the ring, Rod MacMillan told me something. He said that one time he walked in on Mawson, the psychiatrist, in the room with Eugénie. She was asleep and he was touching her. Erotically.'

'So *that*'s what he was uneasy about. Afraid about.'

'He said Mawson swore it had never happened before and would never happen again. MacMillan told him he wouldn't report it to anyone. You know, Carl, it doesn't have to mean anything.'

'Mawson.' He sighed. 'Christ, what next? Anyway, I'm going to try the graphic approach. It may lead to something.'

Tate stood up. 'And I'm going to deliver this ring to the *Banner*. Maybe they'll get something in tomorrow's paper.'

Pedersen smiled. 'I'll have it all solved by tomorrow.'

'Just in case you don't,' Tate said.

CHAPTER 32

'Guess what,' Tate greeted his partner as they entered the building together. He looked glum. They had arrived early, both of them, and parked alongside each other. 'I had a phone call last night from that nurse. The computer's been overhauled and is functioning; she said I could come by and check the lists. She was on night duty and said she'd help.'

Pedersen stopped. 'What did you find out?'

'That nurse wasn't Eugénie at all.'

'What?'

'She was Henriette, Henriette Bouchard. The nurse was in an agony of apology. Apparently she has a thing with French names. So Eugénie was not, to our knowledge, a nurse at Bay Cove.'

Pedersen laughed. 'It doesn't matter. I had a brainstorm. Come into my office for a minute.'

Tate closed the door behind him, his face troubled. 'Yes?'

'What,' Pedersen said, 'if E/J were Ernest/Jane.'

Kay put down the receiver with a crash. Now they wanted her at headquarters; what would be next? She wondered if life was ever going to return to normal.

Whatever normal was. It had occurred to her that maybe Bob, too, was having second thoughts about their arrangement. He might have settled for a more conventional relationship with some other woman; God, she hoped not. At forty-eight she did not welcome being deserted, especially if men like Lewis were all she had to look forward to. She had tried to see his kinkiness as amusing and naughty, but she had never succeeded. And the last time he had come close to hurting her—let's face it, had hurt her. She shivered.

She'd go to headquarters, humour this detective, and then maybe she'd get out of town herself, take a little trip, put all this behind her. And if her husband returned—as he must, eventually; he wasn't about to walk out on his job—she'd talk to him about another sort of marriage. After all, she had stuck to him through all they'd done together and separately because, basically, she liked him. Damn it, loved him!

Assuming, of course, that Detective Pedersen would permit her to leave town. She sighed and went into the bedroom to change her clothes. To go to headquarters, where she had been told she was needed.

*

Roy had been catching up on bill-paying, but thinking ahead to the evening. Dinner someplace pleasant, relaxed—a pot of steamers in one of the little places in the seaside village five miles out of town. Afterwards a stroll on the espla—But all plans were out. He was to appear at headquarters. The invitation had been something more, although it had no actual legal force behind it. He was needed, he had been told. Needed? For what? He wished to God the whole thing were over.

Stanley had to phone Martha to cancel dinner. 'I'm needed at headquarters,' he explained. 'It may not take long, but don't wait dinner. I'll come by afterwards.' She had let him sleep with her the night before and now she sounded soft, welcoming.

'I may have something good to tell you, Stanley,' she said, her tone seductive. He glanced down and could actually see his heart thud in response.

'Martha,' he said. He could think of no other words. 'I'll see you as soon as I can.'

Dr Lewis Mawson was furious. 'Need me for *what*? What have *I* got to do with this investigation? I can see your stopping by to ask about old patients, but I see no sense whatsoever in my coming to headquarters.' But in the end he agreed. Somehow refusing made him appear to be involved. He didn't want that.

Suzanne gave them the information they asked for, the name of the family dentist. 'We've used him forever. Actually I guess he's getting a little old, but he's still practising.'

She was puzzled but perfectly agreeable about coming in to headquarters. 'Have you new information?' She heard the fear in her voice. What was the matter with her? She wanted her mother's murderer found, didn't she? Mentally she shook herself and said brightly, 'Of course. I'll be there.'

*

Oliver Winter was the most reluctant. 'You can't need my help. I have no help to give you. You've learned everything from me that I know about Ann and about Ann's death.' He added, more severely, 'Can't you let us put this behind us? You seem to forget we have feelings about this loss.'

In the end he succumbed, actually, he supposed as he put down the receiver, because he had no choice. Maybe this would be the end of it. He so much wanted this to be the end of it.

'We've brought you all here,' Pedersen said, after the last of them had been seated in the now crowded office, 'because we have a theory and we think you can help us check it out.'

Stanley stiffened and Kay felt her stomach tighten. Roy and Ollie both shifted in their chairs. Lewis Mawson stubbornly looked away.

'Our theory is—' Pedersen paused for effect—'that your sister Jane and Eugénie were one and the same person.'

His statement was met by a shocked silence.

CHAPTER 33

No one spoke for a few seconds. Then Suzanne said, 'Aunt Jane died from cancer nearly ten years ago.'

Kay, who seemed not to have heard her, said, 'Eugénie? You mean that bag lady?' Pedersen wondered if her shock at the idea was genuine.

'Yes, the bag lady.'

'That's ridiculous!' Ollie sounded personally affronted.

'Jane died over nine years ago,' Stanley explained, enunciating as though he were talking to a retarded child.

'We know that's the story,' Tate said.

'The story!' Roy was indignant. 'Her body was identified.'

'I thought Aunt Jane died from cancer,' Suzanne said.

'Mistakes have been made in identification,' Pedersen pointed out.

'I—what on earth makes you think such a thing?' Kay's voice sounded unnatural to her.

'It explains so much. The information she had that was the basis of her letter, which she described to someone as a "surprise". Her statement to another street person that she could have all the money she wanted if she'd just make a phone call. Other things, like her writing to Ann in the first place.'

'I'm completely confused,' Suzanne said.

'Do you *know* that she wrote to Ann?' Roy's tone was contemptuous. 'Or is this just another "theory"?'

'Mr Winter—' Pedersen nodded towards him—'informs us that Ann received a very disturbing letter around the time that Eugénie borrowed paper and pen and a stamp from a librarian and wrote the letter she said would be a "surprise".' Pedersen turned to Kay. 'Didn't she discuss it with you? I understand you shared confidences.'

'Well, this was one we didn't share. She never said a word.'

'Please.' Suzanne stood up. 'Will *somebody* explain to me?'

Pedersen explained. 'You see,' he finished, 'the family originally were just honouring your aunt's wishes. Then she drowned and they couldn't very well explain that she'd been in a psychiatric hospital all along. Also they were protecting you, Miss Ford. Suicide isn't easy to live with.'

'Sue. Please. Mother never told us anything of this. But she did—I told you—act awfully odd around street people the last couple of weeks.'

'Perhaps she was trying to find out what their lives were like. The night of her death she was reading a book called *Ironweed*.'

'A book about vagrants living in the nineteen-thirties,' Tate contributed.

'Coincidence,' Stanley said.

'Which of you identified the body nine years ago?'

'Roy and I,' Stanley said, indicating his brother.

'No,' Roy put in. 'You did. I came later.'

'Well then, you came later.'

'The body had been moved by then,' Roy reminded his brother. 'Taken away.'

'Then I—' Stanley said, his mouth twisted into a wry grimace—'am the culprit. I identified her. It was Jane, I'm positive.'

'The body had been in the water two weeks?' Pedersen asked, his voice gentle.

'Yes. I—it was . . . bloated. That was why I didn't want Kay and Ann to see it. I did identify it and by the time Roy got there, it had been removed for autopsy.'

'Bloated bodies are hard to identify. Features become altered. How was she dressed?'

'She had on—God, I can't remember. It was *nine* years ago!' Stanley ran his hand over his face.

'Let's assume you identified someone you *thought* was your sister. Where do you assume your real sister would have been for the next seven years?' He looked around the group.

'I don't see why I'm here,' Lewis Mawson said suddenly.

'Nor I,' added Oliver Winter, his tone aggrieved.

'You were, respectively, the confidants of Ann and Kay. You may know more about this than you think.'

Suzanne looked at the two men with speculation. Winter shrugged, sighed deeply and turned his head away.

'If Jane was really the bag lady, I guess I mean if the bag lady was really Jane, and had told Ann, Ann certainly would have told us and welcomed her home.' Roy spoke as though that should not need explaining.

'It would seem so. But you tell me she didn't. Did she confide in any of you?'

No one said anything.

'There were other considerations,' Tate put in. 'Perhaps Eugénie wanted financial support. In fact, it would seem very likely that she did. Or some part of your father's inheritance.'

'Would she even have known about it?' Kay asked.

'She had been in Bay Cove for two years before she wrote to Ann,' Pedersen said.

'Before you *assume* she wrote to Ann,' Roy put in.

Pedersen nodded. 'Why two years? And where had she been for over seven years?'

Suzanne spoke up. 'Couldn't Aunt Jane—if it was Aunt Jane—have still been sick?'

'We think that. But we have no way of knowing. We haven't yet checked hospitals in San Francisco and San José. We wanted to talk with all of you first.'

'Why wouldn't Mother have just taken her in? Knowing my mother, I'd think that she wouldn't have been able to go another day thinking Aunt Jane was on the street.'

'She may have been suspicious, thought this person was a fraud, not really her sister.'

'Her name was different.'

'Not so very different. Jane. Eugénie. She may have liked the slightly more elegant name. Your mother never liked her name, did she?'

'How do you know that?'

'I surmised it. She named her children very differently.'

'She told me once that she'd never saddle one of us kids with such a plain name as hers. But I hate the name Suzanne. Why not plain Susan? That's why I use Sue, Suzanne sounds so—affected.'

'All right, Sue, let's get back to the topic under discussion. We haven't all night.' Roy's irritation was evident.

'Sorry.' Affronted, she retired into the background.

'So here we are, with our theory,' Pedersen said. 'The only person in the room who has seen the mysterious letter Ann received is Mr Winter.'

'If Ann wanted it kept from the rest of us, I think her wishes should be respected,' Stanley said.

Winter was looking at Pedersen, a new expression on his face. 'Where does your theory go next? How do you account for the murder? The murders, I mean?'

'Someone,' Tate said, 'didn't want Jane's identity revealed.'

'That's right,' said Pedersen. 'So he—or she—killed Eugénie. Jane, that is. And, because he didn't want Ann recognizing his or her involvement, killed Ann.'

Suzanne's gasp was loud in the silent room. 'You mean one of *us* killed Mother?'

'Or someone acting for one of you.'

'That's—' she looked at the faces around her—'that's impossible. *Why?*'

'Perhaps because of the disgrace. Your aunt was an unstable street person.'

'Or, more likely,' said Tate, 'for money.'

'But what money? You mean money to take care of her? Mother would just have taken Aunt Jane to live with her.'

'Perhaps she wanted to share in your grandfather's inheritance.'

'But he didn't know . . . Although,' she went on in a thoughtful voice, 'he said in the will—'

Kay broke in. 'Really, Suzanne, you're getting into matters that don't concern you.'

'Don't concern me? My mother's death doesn't concern me?'

'I meant—oh, go ahead. Of course it concerns you.'

'All I was going to say, Aunt Kay,' Suzanne explained in her reasonable way, 'was that Grandfather did say in his will that he left his money to "my children". Mother said he worded it that way years ago and never named them. Grandmother had her own money,' she explained to Pedersen and Tate. 'Mother thought he might even have written the will before you were born, Aunt Kay, and worded it that way in case he died before you arrived. That was all I was going to say.'

Someone in the room moved abruptly.

'Then,' Oliver Winter said, 'Jane would have been eligible to collect her fifth of the inheritance. Quite a bit of money.'

'Yes, she would,' Pedersen said. 'Are you having second thoughts about letting us in on that letter?'

'She did tell someone else about that letter,' said Oliver Winter. 'A member of her family. She told me.'

'*You* wouldn't have had a motive for murdering Ann?' Pedersen's tone was conversational.

'I? I loved her. And all I know about this bag lady is what I learned from the letter. I'd better tell you what was in it. I can't remember the exact wording, but the letter said something like this: "I'm writing you because I've come back. I ran away and then was sick for a long time, but lately I've been better and it's time for me to come home. Even though you did the worst thing anyone has ever done to me, marrying Ernest, you've always been my favourite person in the family and I'm turning to you. You needn't take me in or anything, but I just read in a newspaper that Daddy is the *late* Joseph Potter, so he must be dead. I want my share of his money and then I'll go off by myself and leave you alone. I've been living on the street. Get in touch with me under the name Jane Potter at General Delivery. Jane." Ann said she had to find a way to check whether the woman was really Jane, but she wrote her that she'd be in touch and sent her two hundred dollars in cash.'

'Why do you say Ann told someone in the family?'

'She said she did. She said she was going to, rather. She was very much upset about the whole thing.'

'Well?' Pedersen looked around the room, his face pleasant. 'Which of you was it?' He thought he already knew.

'Not me,' said Roy. 'She never said a word to me. But then she wouldn't.'

'Nor I,' added Kay hastily.

'She didn't tell me,' said Suzanne. 'Obviously.

'That seems to leave you, Mr Potter,' said Pedersen, turning to Stanley.

Stanley stood, upsetting a stack of books. 'You have only their word for it.' Then he slumped back down into his chair. 'All right. Actually, Ann did say something to me. I guess I should tell you. It was a trivial reference, really, she was mostly trying to find out if I could have made a mistake in the identification. She didn't go into the rest, the letter from Jane.'

Pedersen swung around to Lewis Mawson, who sat, lips compressed, unspeaking. 'You did a surgical rotation, I assume, as part of your medical training.'

'What—' The physician drew himself up. 'Are you suggesting that I knifed those two women?'

'No. I was merely asking a question.'

'A question! I don't like its implications. Of course I did a surgical rotation.'

Suzanne suddenly spoke. 'That seems pretty silly to me, Detective. Anyone could have . . . done that to Mother.'

'Not anyone,' said Pedersen. 'I, for example, wouldn't have known how to strike a single blow that so precisely found the heart. And two such blows . . .'

'But I mean anybody who had any medical training. Uncle Stan studied medicine. Does that make him a killer?'

Pedersen turned to Stanley Potter. 'You studied medicine?'

'It was nothing, I never did anything with it.'

'But,' Roy said levelly, 'you completed an internship.'

'So I completed an internship. I've never practised. That was years ago, one of my bad beginnings.' He turned to Pedersen, his tone light. 'I always say I'm the living illustration of that old rhyme that goes Doctor, Lawyer, Merchant, Chief. I also started a law programme. And I suppose you'd say I ended up a merchant.' He laughed. It was not a comfortable sound.

'Mr Potter, did you do a surgical rotation?'

'Yes—æons ago. It must be thirty-five years. You don't think I retained the skill to—' He broke off at the detective's face. 'For Christ's sake,' he said, 'you don't think I'd be idiot enough to leave the Carson stickers on those knives if I'd done it?'

'The *Carson* stickers? The name of the store where the knives were bought was never published.'

Everyone in the room had turned to Stanley.

'I—I'm sure I read it. Or it was just a guess. Maybe I saw it when I found Ann. You don't think I'd kill my own sister, the sister I loved—' He buried his head in his hands. 'My own sister—' her said brokenly. Tears poured down his face. 'You don't think—' He raised his ravaged face. 'I miss her so,' he said.

CHAPTER 34

'For a hundred thousand dollars? You mean he killed *two* women for a hundred thousand dollars?' Freda couldn't believe it.

They were having their evening drink. The room was darkening in the dusk, but they had not yet turned on lights.

Pedersen raised his eyebrows. 'That's so little?'

'No, I mean not to us it wouldn't be. But for a murder—*two* murders—as a motive, yes. He could have borrowed it.'

'That's true. And it does seem like little. It was what he would have had to come up with as his share of Jane's inheritance. He couldn't have taken it out of the business again; even if he could have, he'd never have been able to bring himself to do that. You don't understand, Freda, what that prestige in the company meant to him.'

'A job in a software company?'

'Come on. He was a man who had failed at everything he had undertaken for close to forty years. He had finally made it, an executive, looked up to. He panicked. But I think his motive for the murder was not so pure as all that. I think he'd hated his sisters. He'd hated his mother for abandoning him in the way she did and his sisters for so easily gaining his father's approval. Jane, especially. We'll never know whether he really believed his identification of her as the drowning victim—he says yes, but it's clear he wanted her dead, had seen her as his particular enemy all those years.'

'Why? And what do you mean, he'd been failing at everything for forty years?'

'You have to understand the background. It seems Jane was born within two years of his birth. From that day forth his father focused on her. His mother sounds pretty flaky, I doubt that she consistently focused on anything except maybe having another baby. Stanley probably felt ordinary sibling rivalry, but I suspect as one sister after the other got the approval from his father that he so desperately wanted, Jane became a sort of symbol to him—of all the rejection he felt. Then, shortly after Kay was born—the last child—his mother committed suicide. The ultimate rejection.'

Freda arranged a cushion behind her back. 'Odd that the only one to become unstable was Stanley. You'd think Kay—'

He frowned at her. 'I wouldn't say Jane was stable.'

'Of course not. That was an idiotic thing for me to say. Go ahead.'

'When Stanley reached adulthood, he went to college and finally, after much disgusted effort on Papa's part, was accepted by a medical school. He hadn't been outstanding as a student in college. He survived medical school and almost made it through an internship but he edged through all the way. Towards the end he was warned to stick to a safe specialty, nothing diagnostic and not surgery. At that point he decided he'd had it with medicine and dropped out. After an interval of soul-searching, he entered law school.'

'Where he flunked out.'

'You guessed it.' Pedersen swirled the vermouth in his glass. 'I gather rather thoroughly. Then he drifted through a number of other false starts, tried acting, then a design school. And finally ended up selling. Then he heard of a job in a big local software business, the selling end.'

'He must have been pretty old by then.'

'He was. I have the impression that he wasn't much respected there till he began to pour money into the place. Finally he dumped his share of his father's inheritance into the business. That did it. It must have been an exhilarating experience for him, being deferred to and treated as an important person in the firm. And from something he said when he made his statement, I gathered at last he had a thing going with a woman, too.' He paused. 'All down the tubes.'

'And you don't think he deliberately identified the wrong body when that drowned woman was washed ashore?'

'I don't know. He never let any other member of the family see the body, so he must have known at some level it wasn't Jane. Maybe not, though. We believe what we want to believe.'

The room had become dark. Freda reached beside her and turned on one lamp. 'What's the story on Eugénie?'

'We don't know. Maybe she just lived on the streets all those years. Apparently she spontaneously began to get better and decided to come back to Bay Cove. But not home, yet. Strange, some of them become almost . . . professional street people, if you can believe it.'

'I can. You must get so you don't want the demands of normal life.'

'I'm harbouring an incipient vagrant in my house?'

'I won't be leaving right away. But I can understand. At the same time, there must be a longing for home and all that means.'

'I think a longing and a fear. By the time you've lived on the streets for a while, especially a woman of her age, you must feel you just can't make the grade again. I don't know. I'm just guessing, but it seems that way to me.'

'Then she saw something in a newspaper about her father?'

'In the letter to Ann she said she had seen a reference to the *late* Joseph Potter. She realized he must have died. He was a well-heeled gentleman. Maybe she saw it as her chance to make a new beginning. With money, she could escape the demands of family and do it on her own terms.'

'But she was unsure?'

'Probably scared. She must have mulled over the idea for quite a while before she wrote that letter. The autopsy said she was in good health, but the fainting spells may have scared her and got her moving.'

'How did Stanley know about her sleeping in the hospital?'

'After Ann talked to him, he set out to find Jane. Most local vagrants end up spending time on the mall, so he went there, made several trips before he spotted her.'

'And followed her.'

'He hasn't filled in all the details, but I suspect he did. Either just that once or over a period of time until he learned her habits.'

'Then he set out to kill her.'

'And his other sister, yes. Ann.' He added grimly, 'I think he was poorly advised when he was a medical student. He should have gone into surgery.'

She shivered. 'But Ann was the one person in the family whom he really loved!'

'If he did. Something in the way he talked of his missing her made me wonder if he somehow had confused her with his mother. Ann, remember, for all that she was younger, was the mature one in the family, the good one. It sounds as though she may have mothered him; he certainly seems to have needed mothering. If he confused her with Mamma, well . . .'

'He thought he was the only one to whom Ann had shown the letter? He must have planned the murders; he went out and bought two knives.'

'There's something funny about that, too. Why not use a knife from his house or from Ann's? And leaving the stickers on—was that panic or was it ambivalence? Without those identical knives with their stickers, we'd never have connected the two deaths.'

'You're saying he wanted to be caught?'

'Only in so far as all killers who aren't total psychopaths want to. He did kill his sisters when they were asleep; that wasn't just convenience, at some level it was guilt.'

'And he killed Ann because she would know he had killed Eugénie?'

'Yes. Ann had said she would welcome Eugénie home, would see that she got her share of the inheritance. He felt he had to kill her, she knew he had seen the letter and would immediately guess that he had killed Eugénie. Apparently he had tried to convince Ann that Eugénie was a fraud, had tried to discourage Ann from getting in contact with her. Unsuccessfully.'

'Tragic,' Freda said severely. 'Tragic all around. But of course he *wasn't* the only one to whom Ann had shown the letter.'

'No, Winter knew, but apparently never connected Stanley or any other family member with the murders. He knew Eugénie might be Jane, but he didn't want to—besmirch Ann's memory by suggesting an association with them. So he vociferously—and snobbishly, I thought at the time—denied that Ann could possibly have known of a bag lady.'

'How did the rest of the family respond when they realized Stanley had done the murders?'

'Suzanne was horrified, but the others were strange. They sort of shrugged Stanley off, as though he were of no consequence to them. No wonder he always found it rough going in that family. I think they're *all* sick.'

'But feeling sorry for him—I mean understanding what shaped him, that's no reason for—'

'I didn't mean it was.' He looked fondly in her direction. 'You look lovely in that half-light.'

'What? Oh, you look lovely, too.'

'*Lovely?* Men are supposed to look dashing and handsome. And virile. Not lovely.'

'Well, then,' she said, rising to go start dinner, 'you look dashing and handsome and virile.' She looked at him with affection. 'And lovely. Come help.'